THE EIGHTH COMMANDMENT:

The Slow Death
of
Local Journalism

John T. Hourihan

Aster Press
Blue Fortune Enterprises LLC

This book is a gem. This story of a young Irish boy trying to understand the seeming difference between religion and reality is laugh out loud funny. But you don't have to be Irish or Catholic to enjoy this nostalgic journey into the past as he struggles to do the right thing.

Patti Gaustad Procopi, author of *Please… Tell Me More, I'll Get By* and *Stop Talking*.

As a fellow writer of semi-autobiographic fiction, I applaud John Hourihan's new book, *Baltimore Catechism*. Told with the innocence of childhood and the tongue-in cheek irony of adulthood, the book brings out the conflict between religion and reality. Through the eyes of a young Irish-American boy, the book explores what it means to be religious. The author's sardonic whit, coupled with his poignant visual, auditory and olfactory images of people, places and events, makes the book an enticing read. This book is a paean to our common humanity and to what is good in all of us.

Christian Pascale, author of *Memories Are The Stories We Tell Ourselves*, *Poetry of Wonder*, and *Windows of Heaven*.

From the Baltimore Catechism

*"Q. 1306. What are we commanded by the Eighth
Commandment?*
*A. We are commanded by the Eighth Commandment to
speak the truth in all things and to be
careful of the honor and reputation of everyone.*

"Q. 1307. What is a lie?
*A. A lie is a sin committed by knowingly saying what is
untrue with the intention of deceiving.
To swear to a lie makes the sin greater, and such swearing is
called perjury. Pretense, hypocrisy,
false praise, boasting, etc., are similar to lies."*

CHAPTER ONE

Printer's Ink

To tell the truth, to Kevin O'Connor, his country was never so young as when, in the early 1950s, his older twin sisters walked him to Valentino's neighborhood store to buy two eggs, a can of milk, and a pack of his mother's Raleigh cigarettes with money that had been found down the side of the couch.

She smoked Raleighs because they came with a coupon on the back that she would save until she had enough to get towels and washcloths for free. When you've got five kids and are splitting your husband's paycheck with the Brass Rail, that's what you do to survive in rural New England in the time of Eisenhower, the baby boom,

Little Rock, the town elections, the police log, and the Mass schedule at the Catholic Church.

It was at a time when a nickel bag was penny candy, newspapers were papers filled with news, children learned how to duck and cover to stay safe from a nuclear event at school (does anyone remember those fun moments of hiding under a desk), and everyone in this Catholic enclave of Halford knew that "Thou shalt not lie" was the eighth commandment.

To seven-year-old Kevin, Valentino's wife, who helped run the store, was an old woman in her forties. And Valentino was even older. In his time, the old man had seen spittoons, horseless carriages, the legitimization of the press, women getting the vote, and the invention of TV.

But a big part of Kevin's world was this trip to the Congress Street Market, owned by the old couple.

The trips would usually begin with his mother making tea and realizing she had no canned milk. She'd rummage through her purse for a dollar bill or look under the cushions of the Morgan chair or the couch for enough change, and his sisters, referred to only as "the twins," would be sent as his guardians to "the store."

The store was a mile or so away from his house,

although it felt like a year because they had to get by the Delorme's German shepherd and the Allegrezza's cows, but it was a good walk because at the end was a prize.

As they stepped inside from the searing white light of the morning sun, the one-room neighborhood store went black.

Kevin's pupils dilated and his eyes refocused. First, he could see the dark-brown plank floor, wide boards like flat wooden steps leading through a gauntlet of shelves full of dusty groceries, and then his eyes focused on the glass-enclosed candy case straight ahead.

Penny candy was arranged and piled inside the glass-encased counter, rows of neatly separated Maryjanes, Squirrels, Tootsie Rolls, Dots, Crows, Mint Juleps, and then the cat, and after the cat was the five-cent stuff, like Necco Wafers, Waleecos, Mounds and all the stuff he never got unless his father Brendan bought it from the machine at the bar on his way home as a sort of sweet apology for those still waiting for him. At that time, Kevin's mother would meticulously carve the candy into five equal strips for consumption. It was okay because candy bars were bigger then.

The glass front of the candy case was old, curved, and yellow, and it distorted everything inside.

As the old gray cat would get up and begin its slow trek across the case, it looked as if its shining back was rippling as it stretched. Then it would lie back down, and Valentino's old wife would shoo it away so she could let the three children see all the candy all at once.

She was proud of her candy case.

After they had gotten the can of milk, the cigarettes, and maybe an envelope of lime Kool Aid, the children were allowed to spend a nickel on candy, which, in those days, filled a small brown bag. While his sisters were deciding on the candy, Kevin would run his fingers over the morning newspapers in a pile on the floor next to the case. After he rubbed them, he could put his fingers to his nose and smell the most delightful smell in the world.

Printer's ink was the lifeblood of the local newspaper and, in some ways, of the town.

Decades later, he would still remember seeing the black etching of a baseball player on the front page, with the rows of type and the thick black masthead: HALFORD BEACON.

In the neighborhood store, he would sit next to the pile while his sisters talked with Mrs. Valentino.

The smell of cigar smoke, provolone, aging fruit, and printer's ink got into his blood.

Once, a year or so later, his little league team took a tour of the Halford Beacon, and he smelled the same thing there, mingled with cigarette smoke and the heavy aroma of strong coffee. He felt at home here.

Kevin began working for that paper when he was in his early twenties, just after he had returned from the war in Southeast Asia.

The rapid-fire click of the teletype and the roar of the press were the magic that produced an adversary to a government selling an ill-advised war to an unsuspecting people.

Kevin O'Connor was proud to be part of the hometown rag that had said in 1969, while he had still been ankle-deep in Pleiku mud, "End The War Now!"

But then the world flew at jet speed through offset printing, four-color process, jet presses, furniture store and new car inserts, computers, no smoking in the newsroom, no drinking in the newsroom, no swearing in the newsroom, and then his heart broke when it occurred to him that soon there would be no more newsrooms.

The blood was being sucked out of them. The vampire corporate advertisers were draining them of their integrity and replacing it with the will to survive at all costs. Truth had become a secondary requirement that wasn't even required. The public's TV-fed thirst for over-the-top drama and sensationalism dictated the script of altered news stories. They seemed not to care at all what it was replacing.

The transition had begun its descent into the undead wasteland of the internet.

"Get it first. It doesn't matter if it's right. We can fix it later." Later, when no one is looking because they had already seen the wrong version and believed it to be right.

Toward the end of a long, productive career, while working for a major city paper, O'Connor heard a weekend editor say that on the phone to a reporter who was on her way back to the newsroom. She had the rudiments of a story about a fire in the city. The Monday paper was being laid out, and the weekend editor was telling her to just get the story onto her blog before anyone else had it. Luckily, she could do that from her phone as she was driving. There were no three sources, no documentation, and she might have it all wrong. The fire might have been set. It might have taken too long for the fire trucks to arrive. It might have been a building with no smoke alarms. Some people may have been killed. Some may be homeless. But none of that mattered, apparently, and he told her, "Just get it on your blog. If it's wrong, we'll fix it later. No one will know the difference."

People didn't seem to care anymore about sources and documentation, and Kevin felt older than, and as useless as, duck-and-cover.

He was divorced and married again and the father of two adults now, and kids younger than his own children began talking down to the men and women who remembered far in the recesses of their memory the smell of printer's ink and the true purpose of a hometown newspaper.

A new generation of journalists told those who remembered what it meant to be the adversaries to government how they could all blog, how they could put their half-finished stories online.

A flick and a flicker and multicolor pictures of airhead heiresses and short celluloid superheroes and more opinions than Carter has little liver pills lit up across our screens with all the credibility of a Daffy Duck cartoon.

But Kevin O'Connor, at sixty years old, sat at a daily newsroom meeting only a short time before he retired, and he looked out the window wondering if they were doing the right thing.

Is more money and maintaining jobs enough of a reason to jump from the credibility of the Fourth Estate to the brazen conjecture of the internet, where you can find every thought in the universe but nothing proven? So many opinions, but so little truth. Where you can find every filth and depravity ever conceived but so little morality. Where you can find so much typing but so little writing.

In the chill of that morning meeting, his retirement-age-self felt particularly young, except that he had never been so young as when he went to Valentino's convenience store for his mother's cigarettes.

Kevin sat in that newsroom meeting. He had progressed over the years between 1971 and 2006. He was now a mainstay at the daily meeting of a large city newspaper in Connecticut with somewhere near 100,000 readers. He was the wire editor and an opinion columnist. His job was to decide what state, regional, and worldwide news would be put into the paper each day, and then he got to give his opinion about it on Sunday. This meeting was where the contents of the paper for the next day would be discussed and decided on, and Kevin looked out the window and wondered if he was doing the right thing to help it survive.

This morning he felt particularly young, except that the truth that penny candy cost a penny didn't exist anymore, duck and cover was a thing of the far past, and newspapers were on the verge of going the way of the spittoon.

But he still remembered the smell of the printer's ink on his fingertips.

It was something that would never be found on the internet.

It was the smell of truth. It was the admonishment from a fanatic editor: "Find three reliable sources on this and get back to me!" or "Show me the documentation," or "This is a fucking daily newspaper. Don't tell me what you did yesterday. What do you have for today?"

Kevin's daydream ended with the very loud, "Okay" of one of the City Tribune editors.

"Okay," he said again, louder to quell the murmur of the others in the room. "There's a problem in the world that began with death threats leveled at an editor in the Netherlands who printed a cartoon of Muhammed. Since Muhammed's likeness is not supposed to be printed anywhere according to the religion, some Muslims have decided to have the editor killed."

O'Connor tore his eyes away from the view of the building across the street, the city courthouse, and scanned the people in the room. There were ten people sitting around the conference table. Everyone there was in charge of something.

"What does that have to do with us?" a young computer technician asked.

Kevin turned from the window and took a good look at him. The boy speaking was young, too young to remember Murrow, Cronkite, or even Dave Garroway. He was tall and thin and had recently grown a fledgling mustache that, like its owner, was struggling to become meaningful. He had shaved his head rather than suffer the truth of early pattern baldness in his mid-twenties.

Kevin decided to answer him.

"A religion is telling us we don't have the right to print the truth. We can't let that happen," he said. He thought his words would be understood. He thought for sure most of the people in the room would agree with what he had said. This was, after all, an American newspaper, and that meant it had the freedom of the press to tell the truth.

"Big deal," the young man shot back.

"It is a big deal," Kevin answered.

"Why?"

"Because we're the Fourth Estate. We're one of the checks and balances that keep people from operating in secrecy. We tell our readers what is going on in the world. We have to be allowed to tell the truth. People should be able to expect us to tell the truth. We should print that cartoon, large, front page and above the fold, with an apology to Muslims and an explanation of why it had to be done."

"So, what happens if we do?" he asked. The smug expression on his face showed he believed he knew the answer, and he expected the answer would be that nothing would happen, that it wasn't that important. Religion wasn't important, death threats weren't important, the first amendment wasn't important.

"We don't know," Kevin said, leaning closer to the table. "It could be nothing. It could be protests out in front of the building. It could be someone being hurt or even killed."

"So, we don't do it," the young man answered and laughed in Kevin's face. "That would be just stupid. I don't want to put up with that crap just to come to work."

"You've heard of freedom of the press, right?" Kevin asked.

One of the other editors stepped in. "It isn't that easy a decision," he said.

This editor was Kevin's age or a few years younger.

There was a difference, however. Kevin had often wondered if Thaddeus, the new speaker, remembered newspapers being printed on a letterpress, or the yellow teletype tape being regurgitated from its ticker machine. He settled on the hope that his colleague did, at least, remember stories about it.

"We are bound to tell the truth. Well, all the truth that matters. This has been going on for about a year, and it is going to be difficult to tell the truth of this story without showing the picture of the cartoon."

"Bound?" the younger man asked. "What *binds* us?"

"Integrity!" Kevin nearly shouted. Then lowered his voice. "Integrity," he said again at a more acceptable level.

The arts editor, who oversaw books and movies, but really only retyped book reviews sometimes sent in by the authors themselves, spoke up from across the table.

"Kevin's right. It used to be that way in the old days."

"Used to be?" O'Connor cut in. "How is it different now? Aren't we expected to tell the truth anymore? And by the way, in the old days, we never told the truth. The entire 1800s were publishers' lies and spin. It took a long time to get people to believe in the press."

"Damn, O'Connor, it's not that important," Thadeus answered. "Times have changed. We aren't a check and balance against the government anymore. We are here to sell newspapers and keep people in their jobs. We are now just trolling for perverts and selling sensationalism. Get with the program."

"Trolling for perverts?" Kevin asked. "I guess you're talking about that picture of the local eleven-year-old in the miniskirt and the halter top on today's front page?"

"Right," he said. "Trolling for perverts. Selling newspapers so old men like us can have a job."

Kevin's attention returned to the fogged-in courthouse.

The cartoon was printed deep inside the newspaper and was barely noticeable at one column wide.

It was only a handful of years before Kevin O'Connor would give up and retire, but for now, he returned his attention to the barely visible cityscape outside the window.

O'Connor thought about the first time, when at the age of twenty-four years, he had stepped into the newsroom of the Halford Beacon in the town where he grew up. It was less than a year after he'd returned from Vietnam. The paper was looking for a reporter, and he needed a job. As the meeting droned on, he sank back into his daydream.

When Kevin left the room after the meeting, he walked

slowly behind the chair of the young bald computer tech. He stopped, turned back, leaned down to ear level and said softly, "Don't you ever laugh at me again, you punk." He smiled, walked out, and went to his desk.

CHAPTER TWO
Joining the Fight

It was 1970, not long before the country began chipping away at the importance of truth, trading it for entertainment.

Kevin O'Connor was twenty-four, a veteran of Vietnam. He had been hired at his hometown newspaper, the Halford Beacon, on a handshake. His pay came in cash inside a small brown envelope. They didn't even know he didn't own a car until his first assignment.

"O'Connor," Derek Weise, the editor of the small-town paper with a circulation of 14,000, shouted from his desk without looking up. He held the phone against his ear with his right shoulder, and Kevin wasn't even sure if he was still talking to him when his boss said, "There's a fire on Bow Street. Get over there!"

Kevin looked around the room. No one was offering any help.

"How?" he asked to the editor's back as the man turned away from him.

"What do you mean, how? Drive, you damn fool!"

Kevin walked to the editor's desk, picked up the car keys from the tray, and started for the door.

"Where the hell are you going with my keys?"

"Make up your mind, Mr. Weise. Either I'm driving to the fire on Bow or I'm not."

"Don't tell me you don't have a car."

"Nope."

"How the hell did you get hired to be a reporter if you don't have a car?"

"I don't know, man. You hired me."

The dark curly haired editor, ten years Kevin's senior, laughed and shooed the reporter off. "Go, get the story. And get a picture." He handed Kevin a camera from his desk without looking away from his typewriter. "And put gas in my car. It takes high test," he added, referring to the premium fuel.

On Bow Street, a young couple who had two very

young kids had lost their apartment to fire, and the landlord was screaming at them for "burning my place."

The red-haired woman huddled with her kids on either side of her and cried. The little girl was sad. The boy was angry. Kevin got a picture of them with the smoke-filled window in the background. The husband stood, face drenched in despair as he was almost listening to the landlord. Finally, the distraught father turned and said, "We didn't start the fire. I think it started in the wall, inside the wall, I think."

Kevin walked to the fire chief who was now supervising his men pulling the hoses back to the truck.

He nodded at the chief and introduced himself. "How'd it start?" he asked.

"Not sure. Looks like an electrical fire."

"Inside the wall?" Kevin asked.

"Most likely. We'll know by this afternoon. You can give me a call at the station."

"How long did it take you to get here?"

"Less than ten minutes," the chief said. "We're right down the street."

"Is it suspicious?"

He looked back at the apartment house. "No, just a fire in an old house."

"How bad is it?"

"No one is going to be staying in there for a while," he said and left.

"Well, at least no one was hurt," Kevin said as he returned to the young couple who were still standing on the lawn in semi-shock.

Kevin asked the father if he had a place to stay, but they did not. The family was new in town and had just moved in a week before. They knew nobody.

O'Connor collected names, wrote down the address of the building, asked about the cost to rebuild, and returned to the newspaper. He wrote the story — who, what, when, where, how, and why — and threw in that the young couple could be contacted by calling him on his phone at the newspaper. Weise told him he was "a dumbass" for doing that, but they got a few calls the next day, and Kevin relayed the information to the young parents who were staying at the Rose Motel for a few nights that the three landlords who had called had places for them to stay. They would get to choose which one they liked.

It occurred to Kevin that there was more to being a small-town reporter than he had thought. It became clear to him that the paper wasn't just an adversary to the government, it was also an ally to the people it served. He was self-satisfied that those two kids would be sleeping in a bed tonight in a new home, and that he had something to do with it. It felt good to have helped.

The next day, as Kevin arrived at work, Weise pointed out, "Fire reporting has come a long way. Reporters used to get paid by how many column inches in the story and how many names of people they got into the paper. You would have gotten paid a buck twenty for six."

That made no sense to Kevin, and he asked about it.

"If your name is in the paper," Weise explained, "you buy the paper, your family buys the paper, so the more names you get in, the more people who buy the paper, the more who buy the paper the more you can charge for advertising, so we used to pay by the name."

"Why did it stop?" Kevin asked, pouring a coffee and searching the empty desks for an ashtray.

"Ask Stan," Weise said and pointed across the room to the copy editor Stanley, who was about the same age as Weise but looked older because of his receding hairline. He had started at the paper as a kid covering American Legion baseball, then had moved up, longevity and loyalty being paramount in the uphill climb at the newspaper.

"Tell him, Stan," Weise said and laughed.

"Because this guy is a stingy son-of-a-bitch." Stan smiled and kept typing.

"I don't understand," Kevin said.

Stan stopped typing and turned his chair to face Kevin. "There was a fire on Central Street, and Weise here sent me to cover it. It was a big fire, so I wrote the story. It went, 'There was a big fire on Central Street last night. No one was hurt. Among the onlookers were… and I listed nearly every name in Milford." He poked his thumb at Derek and said, "That cheap bastard wouldn't pay me, and he changed the rules."

The other reporter, Jed, walked in the front door from outside. "What are we laughing at?" he asked, and Stanley told him. Jed was a tall, distinguished looking man in his forties. He wore a tweed sport coat that had never seen an iron, and a soft gray hat that looked as if it belonged on the set of Dragnet. He took the hat off as he stepped into the room and hung it on a peg in the wall. He had done this so many times before that he never took his eyes off the floor while he hung his hat, walked to the corner, and poured his coffee.

Everyone, including Lucy the typist, whose job it was to retype press releases from local organizations and keep Weise from swearing as much as he wanted to, was looking at Jed's forehead. Kevin later found out that Jed had gotten the crosshatch cut in the center of his head because he got home tipsy last evening and didn't realize the screen door was still closed. He had walked right into it, leaving the hashtag-like wound.

Lucy, the pretty forty-year-old, looked over the top of her eyeglasses and asked, "What happened to your head?"

"Cut myself shaving," Jed answered in a matter-of-fact tone. It was his story, and he stuck to it. He walked to his desk, sat, and sipped from his paper cup of coffee. He looked from face to face, almost daring anyone to ask for further explanation. No one did, so he spun to his typewriter and began his story for the day's paper. It was about a selectman's meeting from the night before.

Jed was a firm believer that a reporter could get more and better information about a governmental meeting by following it up with a visit to the Keg and Flask and talking to those who had run the meeting after they had a few drinks.

"When it's more difficult to make up a lie, they will more often tell the truth," he told Kevin.

The first local government meeting Kevin was sent to cover was in the small town of Birmingdale, fifteen minutes south of Halford. It was a planning board meeting, and it was as boring as it sounded. He had bought an elderly white VW bug with a moon roof for a couple hundred dollars that he had borrowed from an old friend who ran the Green Finance Company, and he drove down to cover his first meeting.

He trudged into the room in the bowels of the Birmingdale Town Hall wearing a U-Mass t-shirt, cut-off shorts and sandals, carrying his pad and pens. In addition to Kevin, there were five other people in the audience and the three board members. The three people at the table took a long hard look at the only person in the room who they didn't know.

"And you are?" the guy in the middle asked.

"Kevin O'Connor," he said. "Halford Beacon. I'm a reporter."

The town official shook his head, smiled, and looked down at his papers. The three members of the planning board seemed to be laughing to themselves as they pored through their notes in preparation for the meeting.

There was talk of zoning changes that had been made by the Zoning Board of Appeals at its last meeting, and Kevin dutifully wrote them down. There was also talk of new rules about how many handicapped parking spaces would be needed at a new convenience store. No one knew, since this idea of being kind to the handicapped was sort of a recent thing. They eventually passed it over.

Then there came something of interest. Kevin decided it would be his lede. While he was wondering why newspaper people misspelled "lead" on purpose, the chairman of the board was pushing for money to resurface the highway going south from the town toward Rhode Island.

"No one likes that road," he said. "It's like a washboard, so everyone goes all the way to Halford to shop. We want people to come here, right?"

A woman behind Kevin said something under her breath that he thought was interesting, so when he went back to the newspaper that night, he started looking through old editions on microfilm and found what she had said had been true. She had said, "I'll bet his Rhode Island Chamber of Commerce put him up to this."

He wrote the story that night about the parking spaces and waited for the sunlight of the next day to finish the rest of the story. His morning story would have to wait until he could prove it. When you accuse someone of something, he thought, you should at least be able to prove it. The next morning, he made a few calls and made a photocopy of the old story he had found in the microfilm.

He wrote the story with an explanation as to why the chairman was so intent on resurfacing the road to the south, reporting that the reason given by the town official was because people from his town were going north to Halford to shop. He then added that just south of the Massachusetts town was the state line and the city of Lombard. A better road would make it easier for shoppers to get to the Rhode Island town where the Birmingdale Planning Board chairman was the president of the Lombard Chamber of Commerce.

When he wrote the story and submitted it, Weise came to him, stood at his desk, and demanded sternly, "Documentation."

Kevin handed him the copy of the old newspaper article that backed up the contention as to the two jobs held by the planning board chairman/Chamber of Commerce president, and a map showing the towns and the highway in question. He also had copies of separate articles about his appointment to both boards.

"Sources?" Weise asked as he pored over the article.

"Both other members of the board checked it out and found he was on both boards. I also called the chamber in the Rhode Island town, and the receptionist agreed he was the president."

"Did you tell them you were a reporter? You need to tell them you're a reporter, and you have to tell them you're writing a story on it."

"I did."

"Run It. Good job. No wait, did you get pix of the road?"

"Yes."

"Run it."

He did. The selectman quit the chamber of commerce.

Now Kevin knew what was expected, and he spent months getting documentation, photos, three reliable sources, answering the questions, taking pictures, and writing his stories.

As winter arrived, he was sent to cover the visitation of a local son who was now a State Representative. The local politician was to speak to a crowd about the Vietnam War in front of the town library. He wrote the story that night and when he returned to work the next morning, Weise was waiting for him with a copy of his story.

The first line read, *Under the conflicting banners of 'Peace On Earth' and 'Support Our Troops,' a meager crowd of twelve listened to Representative John Doer talk about supporting the troops in Vietnam.*

"You can't say this," Weise barked at him.

"Why not?" Kevin asked.

"First, because AP says there were more than a hundred people there."

Kevin got up and retrieved the picture taken last night at the gathering. He handed it to the editor.

"Count them," he said. There were twelve people in the picture listening to the representative.

"Well, this lede is just your opinion. You can't put your opinion into a story."

"It's not opinion. Both signs were there."

"Well, it isn't my opinion that they conflict. That's your opinion. Kill the story."

He ran an Associated Press account instead. Kevin was angry, but Derek was the boss. The story was killed. That was Tuesday. By Friday, Kevin found the editor was still upset when he handed Kevin an Associated Press picture of some members of the group, Students for a Democratic Society, a group of college kids who were known mostly for protesting the Vietnam war.

"Write a cutline," he said, "and have it begin, 'Trained to Kill' in bold."

"No," Kevin said. "They aren't trained to kill. Not all of

them. That's misleading."

Weise handed Kevin an AP story that reported that some of the members of the SDS were being trained to fire weapons. Kevin did what he had been told, and he wrote the cutline beginning "Trained to Kill," and passed it on to go into the paper. That afternoon, he was handed another picture that needed a cutline. It was a picture that went with a story written by Jed about the Massachusetts National Guard at the Armory in Halford. Under it, Kevin wrote a cutline that began, "Trained To Kill," in bold.

It went in the paper.

The next morning, Kevin found himself unemployed.

It was 1971. Kevin wouldn't return to working with newspapers for thirteen years. During that time, he would get married, finish college, have a daughter and a son, teach high school English, sell envelopes, be a stay-at-home father, and work a short stint as VP of Purchasing and Production at an office supply business. After all that, he returned to journalism.

———

It was 1984 when Kevin woke up one morning in the upscale town of Hollis. His family of four had been living there for a while now; he and his wife and their two toddlers. His wife didn't like him much, based mostly on the amount of money he wasn't making, and was embarrassed when he decided to complain in the local newspaper about one of the companies in town, a chemical company.

By that time, Kevin had graduated from Framingham State with honors, taught high school English for about five years, and left teaching for what his wife insisted was a "real job" of selling envelopes to businesses. It was a job found for him by her high school friend who worked at an employment office. In his wife's defense, he had been making $9,000 a year as a teacher, and the sales job paid $18,000 in his first year.

One afternoon, fourth grader Sandy and her brother Paul, fourteen months her junior, showed him that the back door of their home had been jimmied while he was at work, and they were at home. They said they had no idea how it happened. He was frightened for his children's safety so, after a lot of deliberation and a few loud arguments with his wife, he decided to become a stay-at-home father. The decision had been made based on which of the parents could make more money. It turned out that the kids had lost the key and decided a screwdriver might work just as well, but he hadn't heard that until well after he had quit his job.

One morning, in the summer of 1984, he looked out the kitchen window into the backyard. The large oak tree that had only yesterday been filled with green leaves was now brown. The flower beds and the lawn were dead and had also turned brown.

Kevin asked around town and found that a chemical company in town had a spill that was mishandled, and the spill had become a cloud of hydrofluoric acid that had floated over part of the town, killing plants and polluting yards.

Nothing more was said by the company for weeks while more of the vegetation in town shriveled.

Looking out the kitchen window over his backyard one afternoon while the kids were at school and his wife was at work, he poured a coffee. He stepped out the back door, walked past the tree house he had fashioned from the remnants of the old shed, and followed the path into the small field behind his land to the raspberries he and his children had picked every morning. The bushes were brown and the berries black and shriveled. The culprit wasn't even a human. It was a company. Kevin decided to do something about it. He poured his coffee out into the brown and dried lawn, turned on his heel, and headed back inside. That afternoon, he went to the local newspaper with a letter to the editor.

It read:

"It took human beings a lot of years to learn not to relieve themselves in the water upstream from where they drink.

"The (chemical company) spill may not have left a hazardous residue, but it certainly left a bad taste in a lot of mouths. It is a sort of aftertaste of a residual taste that builds with each new encounter.

"The first taste was the spill itself, and the manner in which it went unreported; then came the responsibility for the defoliation and the manner in which it went unaccepted. Next, of course, was our explanation by company officials at a town meeting and the manner in which it went unclarified, and then I got a letter.

"The letter read, 'Dear Mr. O'Connor: This is to serve as notification to you that a Professor Gardner has completed his evaluation of your property.

"(He) has submitted his recommendation to us to begin fertilization, which we will implement immediately.

"If there is any reason that you do not wish us to begin fertilization, please contact the company at 1-800-555-0100 as soon as possible.

"Thank you for your patience and cooperation in this matter.'"

Against the wishes of his wife, who wanted to take the fertilizer offer, Kevin called the company to find out why they wanted to fertilize dead plants. He expected that if he took the offer, it would be the last thing the company would do for his family.

He was connected with a man who said that he "runs the place." He explained to Kevin that Professor Gardner, in fact, hadn't finished the evaluation or his report, but he (the man who runs the place) had decided not to just sit around. He wanted to "act fast, get something started right away."

It was difficult not to think about the "lime slurry" the supposed neutralization process that the chemists had said caused the vapor cloud in the first place.

Kevin wrote in his next letter to the editor, "To anyone who can write a letter to me thanking me for my patience and cooperation, I have to explain that the letter isn't worth the very expensive paper that it's written on. I have no patience with people who pollute our land and who did not even report it as regulations demand.

"I have no patience with people who must have lawyers present to explain how they will make right their shoddy safety procedures that put life and property in jeopardy. I have no patience with companies who stand with impudence and do that in our water. And I have no patience with people who put the opportunity of relaxed environmental regulations above their moral obligations to the surrounding homeowners.

"How do you make it right? Come to my home. Ask Me what I want done to rectify the damage, then get it done, and that will be a good start."

When the letter appeared in the paper, his wife was furious.

"They're not going to give us anything now. You just had to open your big mouth. What are we going to do with that dead tree in the back yard? It will take hundreds of dollars to get it cut down and hauled away."

She was right. By writing the letter and having it published, he was running the risk of being the odd man out of any recompense. If he had helped keep it quiet, he might have made some money. While making dinner that night, he worried he had screwed up again. All his life he had tried to live up to his father's expectations that he would be the one to stand up for justice, like his father did when the shoe shops were underpaying his co-workers, but it seemed that every time Kevin did it, he ended up in trouble.

Of course, his father had been fired for bringing in a union to stop the practice, and now Kevin had a sixty-foot-high dead tree in the backyard, the blackberries his kids had picked each morning for breakfast were gone, and he had just called out the deep pockets of the chemical company that could have paid to fix the problem.

His wife was pissed. Kevin was an idealist, and his wife was a utilitarian. They clashed a lot. Then, when there was a response in the paper to his complaint, when someone told him to "get a life," that sewage from his home probably "ends up in Boston Harbor," and Kevin should just take the fertilizer the company wanted to pay for and keep his mouth shut, the tension at home mounted. His wife Karen held off as long as she could before telling him he should have listened to her and kept quiet.

His next letter said: "The astounding possibility that when I flush my toilet, it might wind up in Boston Harbor never occurred to me, but with Reagan's people suggesting that we dump hazardous waste in outer space, I suppose it is a possibility.

"It seems to me that there is a very definite single

standard here in Hollis, as well as throughout the nation, that if a certain practice is profitable enough, if it creates jobs for commercial use on a political ticket, if it helps a friend's business to survive, then it is alright if it temporarily or permanently damages the earth and its environment."

His wife didn't talk to him for about a week, until they got the call from the chemical company.

"What?" she asked after the call as Kevin put the phone down.

"They are going to pay to take the oak tree down and haul it away, and they are going to pay us for the lawn, the flowers, and the berries."

He winked at his daughter, but he knew that the blackberries that they had often turned into jam were not going to grow back, and they weren't even on his property. The blackberries were what had pissed him off in the first place. The damn company had ruined a memorable practice that he enjoyed with his kids. He was sorry that he had angered his wife, but he was also satisfied that the company had to pay more than they had wanted to for messing with his kids.

This situation changed his perspective. Within a few days, it occurred to him that being a stay-at-home dad was fine, but writing in a newspaper was important.

He and his wife, while sharing a joint on the front porch, loudly discussed his going back to work. She agreed they could use the money, but it would have to be part time, and it would have to be at night, so he could take care of the kids during the day. She was a well-respected insurance person and was making more money than he had made as an English teacher.

As a teacher in a public school, his paycheck had left his family eligible for food stamps. It was the reason she had gone back to work in the first place, not really for the money but because of the embarrassment of qualifying for "welfare."

Kevin knew that it wasn't music that calmed the savage beast. It was money. The money would be welcomed, but the money was not why Kevin returned to journalism.

Kevin spent the first morning of his quest to return to work putting together a resume and thinking about what he could answer to the questions he would most likely be asked.

The kids were off to school, his wife was at work, and Kevin had to wait until they were all home and fed before he would finally go to his interview at a local newspaper a few towns over. As he watched the suburban mothers drive by his house on their way to shopping or work, he thought about what he was about to do.

Sitting on the front steps, he drank his coffee and thought. There was power in a local newspaper. Town and regional newspapers told the past, present, and future of their circulation area. Without them, nothing, and no one, would be held accountable for anything unless it was of national or international concern. Good things would go unnoticed, and bad things would remain secret. State and national elections were covered on television and in papers like *The Boston Globe*, but without local newspapers, no one would hear about corruption at the local level. No one would know who needed help or who had helped.

He cleaned the house as time flew by, made dinner, put the dishes in the dishwasher, and for the first time in a while, he put on a sport coat and tie.

"The job is editing the calendar," the young special-sections editor told him as he finished his coffee, crumpled the paper cup, and tossed it into the wastepaper basket beside his desk. "It hardly pays anything. The two center pages of our weekly special section we call the *Extra* are a calendar. Press releases get mailed in. They will all go to you, and you fill out the calendar. Friday's section needs to be done on Tuesday. Want the job?"

He took it. "See you Wednesday," he said, and they laughed that he was giving himself the most amount of time he could have to learn the job and get the first calendar done.

"Smart," Andrew said.

Three weeks into his new job, Kevin noticed the young editor, his boss, walking absently through the newsroom.

"Everything okay?" the boss asked as he approached Kevin's desk, and then he walked off without waiting for an answer.

"Hey," Kevin called after him. "Is there a problem?"

"I need to fill about two pages. A couple of big ads got canceled."

"When?"

"I need the copy by tomorrow."

"Good luck," Kevin said, but he started thinking about a possibility.

The calendar was filled, and it was only Monday. The only responsibility he had for the next day was to type out the stories called in by the stringers in the outer towns. He looked through the press releases that had come in that hadn't been appropriate for the calendar and got an idea. Press releases, written by receptionists and mailed off to the paper, weren't the most often read parts of a newspaper. Kevin realized with a quick rewrite they could be more important to the paper and to the people sending them in.

There were four craft fairs that hadn't made the calendar, and he saw a way to get them some advertising.

He wrote, "It's over the re-routed aquifer and through the industrial complex, to grandmother's condo we go, and it doesn't matter if the horse knows the way we're taking the car. It's faster."

He then explained how the four different towns had for decades hosted craft fairs and their wares had always been perfect locally made gifts for the holidays. He finished a short story about them and moved on.

He read the next press release and typed, "Some actions are special by their essence and some by merit of their longevity. Jonathan Ancher of South Street, Natick, likes to do good things for young people. Many people, of course, have seen the need to do something good for the youth of their town. Ancher, however, has been doing good things for the young of Natick for so many years that some of the 'children' he has helped are approaching retirement age."

Next came, "Most of us have had a Kool-Aid stand,

or sold old comic books, or returned bottles to the store when we were eleven years old, and with the money we might have bought a baseball, or a doll, or splurged on a sundae. The endeavors were fun, but were they enough fun in themselves to have done the work and given the money away?

"Jeff Paladino, of Franklin, is also at that enterprising age. He is eleven, but according to others, his enterprises are mostly for Star Market collecting money for Jerry's Kids. He collected $530 for Muscular Dystrophy."

When all three short articles were finished, he sent them to Andrew's machine.

Within a few minutes, Andrew arrived at Kevin's desk.

"Where did these come from?"

"I wrote them. Some of the stuff that goes into the calendar just warrants a better telling. These people are winners. They deserve to be written about."

With that, a new column was begun for *Extra*. It was called *Winners*.

In the next weeks, the special section told the story about a sixteen-year-old who kept his friend from drowning, a group of parents who used a pile of truck tires to build a neighborhood park, a couple who travelled to China and returned to tell how in 1985 the Chinese were work working diligently and overtime on their high-tech industries. There was a story of a fourth grader, who had phocomelia, and who had partially developed arms and legs and no hands or feet, but who could stand on his head, drive a big wheel, bowl, ski, roller skate, and draw pictures.

Through that column, the local newspaper had taken advantage of press releases for local organizations that so often had ended up in the basket beside the editor's desk with his crumpled coffee cup to illuminate the present of the local people, organizations, and culture.

It felt good to be part of it, and when he was told a few months later how there were now more ads for the *Extra*, and he would not have to produce the *Winners* column anymore, he dug in.

"Did I ever tell you about how newspapers used to pay reporters by how many names they got into a story?" he asked and began to explain. "If your name is in the newspaper, you buy the paper. More circulation gets you more money for your ads, more ads give you more money, and with more money you can buy more paper and ink and hire more salespeople. Putting more names in the paper is profitable."

Someone listened, and the newspaper kept the column.

Then one morning the managing editor of the paper called Kevin at home and asked him to come in to work for a meeting. He got the kids off to school and drove to work.

"We are going to make a concerted effort to put the Halford Beacon under," the managing editor of the city newspaper said. "We are going to go after their advertisers first, and then their circulation." She looked at Kevin and asked, "How do you think we can do that?"

"Me? I don't know," he said.

"You're the only one here who worked there. I thought you might have some ideas. What are their strong points, weak points?"

"I don't know what you mean." He did, but he wasn't sure how much he wanted to say.

"They have like three reporters. That is one of their weak points," she prodded.

"Not really," Kevin said. "They only have three reporters in house, but they have a stringer for every one of the thirteen towns they cover, and each one of them lives in the town they cover, most of them for life. I think it's the opposite. I think their staff is their strength."

"A strong point? How can a part-time staff be a strong point?" She laughed.

"Institutional knowledge," Kevin answered.

"Each one knows the history of his or her own town. Each one went to school with the town officials, or their fathers or mothers. Each one knows who is a crook and who is a good human being. None of them lives in Boston and covers Halford like your reporters do. It isn't a weak point. It's a strong point. It's their strength. You have a woman who moved from Braintree to Oxfield covering Halford. They have a woman who grew up in Halford covering Halford. The woman covering Whitefield for the Beacon graduated from the local school, and nearly every town official is related to her in some way. They have a long-time resident of Hamilton covering Hamilton. Who do you think is going to get a call in the middle of the night from a selectman who wants to break a story?"

"We don't care about that," she said. "We don't care about what they cover. The Beacon is a piddly-assed local paper that has little or no effect on anything. We care about their advertisers."

Kevin didn't agree with her and decided he was on the wrong side.

That night, after a long and loud debate, his wife and he decided the kids were old enough to be latch-key kids again, and he found himself in the publisher's office of the Halford Beacon, in his hometown, where he had first become addicted to printer's ink.

CHAPTER THREE
In Search of Truth

Kevin O'Connor was thirty-nine years old, and he sat at a formidable wooden desk across from the new publisher of his hometown newspaper. This wasn't the publisher who had so long ago fired Kevin. This man was young, in his forties, wore glasses, and seemed very comfortable in his position. He had been chosen for his background in banking, as if someone had known it would take a financial wizard to keep this profession afloat for very long. He sat comfortably back in his chair.

"So," he said, smiling. "What can I do for you?"

Kevin was surprised the publisher had accepted his request to talk with him about a job. The paper had not advertised for a reporter, but here he was.

"Have you ever walked into a bar, and the hair on the back of your neck stands up, and you know you're in the wrong place?" Kevin asked him.

"I don't drink," he said.

"Okay, have you ever suddenly realized you were in a fight, and you were on the wrong side?"

"I have never been in a fight," he said.

"Okay, have you ever had an experienced reporter, college educated, combat veteran, hometown boy come in here and tell you he was willing to be a full-time reporter for you and take about $18,000 a year for his salary?"

Kevin got the job, probably because the median income for a reporter in 1986 was in the mid-twenties.

At first, neither of them even knew what Kevin's job would be. Within days, it was realized that it might be a good idea to remind the people of Halford who they all were. For the first months, Kevin filled the pages with stories of the Irish Catholic school that had closed, the Italian musicians who had played during prohibition in Halford's speakeasies, and the inordinate number of boxers of both nationalities who had come out of the smallish Massachusetts town. The local stories turned, naturally, into a column where Kevin went to coffee shops in different towns and wrote about what was happening there.

Another part of his job for the next few months was to gather the police logs and get into the paper who had been arrested, who had been in an accident, who had too much to drink. Each morning he stopped at the police station, read the log of what had happened the night before, and wrote it up for the paper.

"Why the hell am I doing this?" he suddenly asked one morning from behind his typewriter. He slammed the keys, and they clogged together in a clump. He sat back and lit a cigarette. "I'm not doing this anymore."

"Doing what?" Weise fired back.

"This damn police log. All it does is embarrass people. Just because someone screws up on a Friday night, do we have to run it up the flag for everyone to see?"

Weise finished his own typing and stood from his chair. "Come here. I want you to meet someone."

Weise walked through the newsroom and into the high-pitched whine and oil smell of the press room. Kevin loved the smell of the oil and ink, but not so much the whine produced while the press was idling and waiting for the plates to be attached. He liked it better when the press whirred and clanked to life and produced the truth of the day for the people of Halford and the twelve surrounding towns.

Kevin hustled to keep up with the editor, who seemed to be looking for someone.

As Kevin caught up, Weise was calling to a middle-aged man who had climbed up onto the machine and was tightening bolts.

"Ted," he called. The man waved from the top of the brand-new offset printing press. The young press mechanic had wavey black hair and his dark skin hinted that his roots were in a Middle Eastern country. He jumped down from the machine and smiled. "Hey Derick," he said as he approached, "How is your day going?" His accent cemented the Middle Eastern origin.

"Going good, Ted. Kevin here is having trouble with the police log. Remember the story you told me? About your brother?"

Ted seemed confused for a second, but then understood. "Break time," he said and motioned for Kevin to follow him to the break room. When the two men were seated across the table in front of their coffees, Ted asked, "Have you ever been arrested, Kevin?"

It was obvious to Kevin, from the lines in the corners of Ted's eyes, that he had underestimated the age of the man sitting across from him.

"Yes," Kevin said. "When I was a kid."

"And your name, it was included in the newspaper?"

"Yes."

"How did that make you feel?"

"I was pretty pissed. I was arrested for trying to outrun a cop up at the quarter mile. My parents took my license away and grounded me for a month."

"My older brother was arrested once," Ted offered.

"What for?" Kevin asked.

"He had attended a small rally. You call it a protest. To impress the girl he was with, he wore a peace symbol on his collar. You know the one. It means stop bombing. The circle one?"

Kevin nodded.

"A policeman saw him walking home and arrested him. My family didn't know where he was. My father checked the hospitals that night."

"Wait a minute," Kevin interjected. "He was arrested for wearing a peace symbol? That's bullshit. You can't be arrested for wearing a peace symbol."

"Not here, but in Iraq, where my family lived. They were in Kirkuk, up north in Kurdistan. Do you know where Kurdistan is?"

"No, sorry."

"No matter. My father next checked the morgues. When he didn't find him there, he checked to see if my brother had been impressed into the Iraqi army. We didn't see him again for nearly a year, and when he came home in the middle of the night. He had lost fifty pounds and had no fingernails."

"Oh, bull shit!"

"No, Kevin. Not bullshit. Truth. In some places in the world, the police can arrest you for anything, and your family doesn't even know. Here in the United States of America it is in the newspaper the next day when you are arrested. It is not to embarrass the people arrested. It is to let your people know the police have arrested you, what you were arrested for, when you will go to court, and what your punishment will be." Ted stood up, finished his coffee, and said, "The thing you do in the morning here is more important than you think. It is not for the police. It is for the people you think you are embarrassing."

Kevin returned to his job with a new enthusiasm for the truth.

Then came the tree belt.

In the neighboring town of Faithville, there was a

piece of land called the tree belt.

Between the roads and the sidewalks sat a strip of grassy land about six feet wide. It didn't occur in every part of town, just in parts closer to the center. Sporadically, trees grew in the space, hence the name, tree belt.

It seemed that there had been a funeral, and the wake was held at the family's home. Not wanting to obstruct the narrow roadway, most of those attending pulled their cars up out of the road with the right-side tires firmly on the tree belt.

They were all ticketed. When the police entered the home unannounced and complained that all the cars would have to be moved immediately, they were asked why they had given out tickets in the first place. The answer had been, according to the woman who had called Kevin at the paper, "You were parked on the tree belt. It's against the law."

He had answered the phone on his desk, and the old friend who lived in the town where they both had attended high school asked him for a favor.

"Would you find out what the hell is going on here with this tree belt thing? No one has ever heard of it, and the whole town is getting tickets for being on the damn tree belt," she said. "We always parked there to get out of the road. The roads aren't that wide, you know? Why would we possibly need a law like that?"

On the front page of Saturday's paper, Kevin's column pointed out that, regrettably, there was, in fact, a tree-belt law in Faithville.

Kevin had gone to the source. Inside the front room of the police station, he asked the chief of police where the law had come from, and the chief had produced a piece of paper stipulating that the law said, "There will be no parking on the tree belt," in the town of Faithville.

Since the piece of paper Kevin was handed was on the letterhead of the town administrator, he asked the chief, "Who made this law? Is it a town bylaw? It doesn't look all that official." What he found out—when it was written, where it was penned, and who wrote it—was interesting.

"I was handed this by the town administrator," the chief said. "She hired me, so for me, that makes it a law." He didn't seem to care about when, who, where, what, why, or how. Kevin did.

He had a point, though. If those in town who made the laws and those who enforced them both believed it was law, it was a law. This fact, in and of itself, was important to the townspeople. Kevin asked the town administrator late that afternoon where she had gotten the law and was told, "Do your own research. It's a public document."

After several hours of library research looking over the minutes of old selectmen's meetings in the town library, he found not only the law, but the reason the law was written in the first place. It seemed that the law had been coined in the early 1900s, about eighty years earlier. The Windenmere family ran the town with what some called an iron fist in a velvet glove. Mostly, the family took care of its workers at a time when there were two thousand people living in the town and there were nearly two thousand people working at the Windenmere factory in the town's center.

At that time, the hierarchy at the factory was also appointed to be the town officials. No one bothered to run against them, and if anyone had the temerity to run, the shop would be emptied, and the workers would walk an eighth of a mile down the street to the Town Hall to vote for whoever they were told to vote for and keep their jobs. Rules in town were written by the Windenmere family or their flunkies.

The Windenmeres owned most of the land and nearly all the houses and rented them out to their workers. On Sundays, if the family wasn't having a party at their home, they rode in a horse and buggy through the town to enjoy the New England beauty of their very own fiefdom.

On one occasion, they found that someone else was having a party. It seemed the town's first family hadn't authorized the party to take place, so taking stock of what was happening at the unauthorized party, they had gone home and written a town by-law that had, in fact, stated that "There will be no parking on the tree belt," and it will also be against the law "to throw lobster bodies in the road."

Kevin assumed that the additional crime of "indiscriminate crustacean discardation" had also been happening at the unauthorized party. A law that was a turn-of-the-century punitive rule for a resident for having an unauthorized party was being used to ticket people at a funeral nearly a hundred years later.

In his column, Kevin explained where the law came from and why, and he asked the chief if it was also still against the law to throw lobster bodies in the road.

The chief was unhappy, and he told Kevin, "You don't want to make an enemy of me. I cut my teeth on police work in Arizona, and Phoenix is a lot more dangerous than Faithville." He obviously thought that should scare the New England small-town reporter who graduated from General Windenmere High School.

"Arizona?" Kevin asked.

"That's right," the chief answered.

"Did you ever go down to South Phoenix? Down by South Second Avenue?" Kevin asked.

"Not without backup," the chief said with a laugh.

"That's where I lived," Kevin told him, standing up. "Sorry if the tree belt thing has caused you trouble, I really am, but truth is truth. That's what they pay me to do. Tell the truth."

On Monday morning, when Kevin arrived in the newsroom, Weise was on the phone. As Kevin passed the desk, he heard his boss say, "Buddy, you think O'Connor made you look bad on purpose? You can come on down here and sit in this fucking newsroom for a few days, and then you'll understand, we don't do anything on purpose here. If you're pissed off, that's on you." He slammed down the phone.

Within a few seconds of Kevin sitting down at his desk, he noticed Weise standing beside him. "If you aren't pissing someone off, you aren't doing your job," Weise said, and he stalked back to his desk with a smile.

Kevin put a sign over his desk that afternoon that said, "Piss someone off today," and for about fifteen years, he did, but only on Mondays, Wednesdays, and Saturdays when his column ran.

The police chief wasn't done with the reporter he believed was his new opponent, but there were other police departments around, and as sure as this one in Faithville needed a little sunshine to be shone on it, there was another that deserved a little help.

In Halford, a cop was being attacked by townspeople who were outraged by something he had said to two fourteen-year-old girls. The townspeople were not yet carrying pitchforks and torches, but seemed to be on the verge, and a reporter from Kevin's old newspaper was fanning the flames. The out-of-town newspaper was calling for the officer to be fired if not hanged.

CHAPTER FOUR
Right is Right

⁘

The Halford chief of police had called an urgent meeting in the dimly lit conference room in the basement of the police station, and it wasn't going well.

An officer was under fire from some prominent people in the town for his actions during a discussion he'd had with three high school students.

Fidgeting at the table in the conference room were the chief, the middle-aged officer under fire, Kevin, two photographers, and the reporter from the out-of-town newspaper.

Before the meeting officially began, the other reporter turned on his tape recorder, shoved the miniature microphone toward the officer, and nearly shouted, "You called two fourteen-year-old girls 'sluts'. What do you have to say about this?"

The cop was in his early 40s, heavyset, and looked like someone's father more than a police officer.

"I did not call anyone sluts," the cop answered evenly.

"Are you calling them liars now?"

"No. I'm calling them little girls who are mistaken."

"They told me you called them sluts. I believe them. If you're saying you didn't, then you are calling them liars. It's one or the other. It's black or white."

"Wait a minute," the chief broke in with a stern look. "Turn that thing off."

Chief James Laronga was a formidable-looking man at six feet, two inches and 215 pounds. He worked out every day and looked it. He motioned toward the tape recorder on the desk. "I want to set some rules for this meeting."

The barely out of journalism school reporter begrudgingly hit the off button.

"What rules?" he asked.

"First, keep it civil. Everyone gets to speak. We want to get to the facts of this, not the most sensational version. The facts." The chief looked around the room. Kevin remembered a story he had heard from a friend of his about the now top cop.

Laronga was known to be a man who could cut through any minutia to get immediately to the reality of a situation. The story went that when the chief was a recent high school graduate, he and his friend had gone to their college interview together, and when the interviewer got behind in his schedule, he took them into his office together. The admissions official asked, "Why do you want to go to college, James?" the young man who would later become chief of police in his hometown had honestly answered, "Well, Larry told me we could play football. Is that true?"

The interviewer had stumbled at first, then said, "Yes, I guess it is true."

"Then I'm in!" Laronga said and stood up and left. They both got accepted into the school.

Kevin had to laugh to see who was in charge here, and he wondered if the other reporter knew what he was up against. He respected the young man who had become chief of police, and he knew this man was not about to back down from a reporter. He was honest, fair, loved his town, and protected his people.

"This is not going to be some hatchet job. Officer

Gerardi is a good man. I don't want him assassinated in your newspaper."

"So, you're going to whitewash this thing?" the reporter asked.

"No. We'll get to the bottom of it."

"We'll see," the reporter answered. "Can I turn this back on?" he asked.

The chief looked at Kevin. "Don't you have a recorder too?"

"No. I've done most of my work," Kevin answered. "I'm just here to see if there is anything new. I think I'll be able to remember what is said."

"Go ahead," the chief said. "Turn it on."

The reporter did and immediately attacked again. "You called two young girls sluts. Do you think you should still have a job here?"

The cop looked to his chief.

"Okay," the reporter said, turning toward the chief. "Do *you* think he should still have a job here?"

"Yes," Chief Laronga replied.

"So, you think it is appropriate to call teenage girls sluts?"

"No, I don't."

"Then he will be punished?"

"No. Not without proof."

"But you just said you thought what he said was inappropriate. Why would you keep him on as a police officer?"

"I didn't say that."

"You did. Should I play it back for you?"

"Wait a minute." The chief was clearly upset with the rapid-fire attack. He took a deep breath, pushed his way up from the table and said, "Let's take a break."

"We just started," the reporter protested.

Laronga stood behind his chair. He paused for a second and then started for the door to the hall. As he walked, he motioned for Kevin to follow him. The out-of-town reporter rose too and began toward the hall.

"Not you!" the chief said, pointing at him. "You stay here. Kevin, come with me."

As the two stepped into the hall and closed the door, the chief turned to Kevin, pulled his pistol from its holster, and handed it to the local reporter. "Here," he said. "Take this before I shoot someone."

"The guy's a pain in the ass, isn't he?" Kevin asked and laughed.

"Yes, he is. I'm worried for Dick's job."

This was a serious situation. "Why?"

"I'm getting a lot of calls. People are waiting to hear what is found out. I don't think he did anything wrong. He gave them good advice. He cares. You know he was the cop at the school all last year. He did a great job." He put the gun back in its holster. "What are you going to write about it?"

"I don't know yet, but from what I have heard so far, I have an idea that he didn't call those kids sluts."

"I know but calling a couple of little girls liars might be worse. What do you think?"

"I don't know," Kevin said. "Let's get this over with, and we can figure out the truth."

They returned to the meeting.

The reporter turned on the recorder again, but before he could resume his attack, the chief turned to Kevin. "Do you have anything to say, Kevin?"

"I do. Officer Gerardi, what happened?"

The police officer looked up from staring at his hands folded on the table.

"I gave a talk for DARE at the school. You know the talk. It's about how not to take drugs, and when it was done, the kids all started leaving, but a couple of girls waited behind. They came up to me and said they had a question, so I climbed down from the stage and stood with them. They told me some boys were giving them a hard time. Calling them names, snapping their bra straps, stuff like that. Now, I know it's almost summer, but they were dressed… well, I wouldn't let my girls out of the house like that."

The other reporter jumped in. "Do you think that's a reason to call them sluts? Because of the way they were dressed?"

"No. Not at all. I work at the school. I know these kids. They're good kids, but halter tops and shorts that don't cover much at all—I wouldn't let them go to school that way. I told them the boys were wrong. I would talk to them. I told the girls I would make sure the boys knew they were wrong, and they were to apologize and then leave them alone."

"So, you didn't call them sluts?" Kevin asked.

"No. I told them that the way they were dressed will bring unwanted stuff from people who don't know any better."

"So, you are saying they're liars?" the reporter asked.

Kevin spoke before Girardi could answer.

"What else did you say to them?" he asked.

"I told them that they may not know it, but they were dressing in a way that would attract some not so good attention. One girl said she didn't understand, and I said if you dress like sluts, people are going to think you are sluts."

"You heard him," the reporter said, looking at the chief. "You heard him. Are you going to fire him or what?"

"I'm not going to do anything until I find out the truth here."

"So, now *you're* saying the girls are liars?"

"The meeting is over," the chief said, stood up and left the room. Everyone else followed.

Kevin drove to the school. He went in and headed straight to the guidance office.

The guidance director was a friend of his father's, and Kevin knew he could get the truth from him.

"Do you know this cop, this Officer Girardi?" Kevin asked.

"I do. He was stationed here in the building last year."

"Is he a good cop?" Kevin asked.

"Well, first I don't like police being in the school unless there is a reason, so I didn't really want him here at all."

"Understood."

"But it turned out he was good for the kids."

The guidance director peered for a few seconds over the tops of his glasses at Kevin, then he reached into the center drawer of his desk and handed Kevin a piece of paper. "When you told me on the phone what you wanted to talk about, I jotted down a few names of people you should talk to. They were here last year. Students. They graduated. You should hear what they have to say about Girardi. Ask them how they feel about him."

"What about the girls who said he called them names?"

"They are good kids. Good students. Good families. Like any high school kids, they want to be accepted, so they wear the uniform, and they attract jackasses. Go talk to the people on that list."

———

Later that day, Kevin found the first person on the list. He was a young man working as a maintenance worker in the Town Hall. Kevin saw him on a ladder, cleaning out a heating duct in the hallway. He looked young enough to still be in high school. He wore jeans and a white t-shirt and some very worn brown work boots.

"Are you Gabe Ronson?"

"That's me," the lanky boy with long brown hair said as he descended the ladder and stuck out his hand.

"Hi, I'm Kevin O'Connor from the Halford Beacon. Mind if I ask you a few questions?"

"About what?" the boy asked.

"About officer Dick Gerardi."

"Sure, what do you want to know? I mean, he arrested me once, if that's what you mean."

"No. He is accused of demeaning a couple of young girls because of the way they looked. Some people want him to lose his job. Do you think that sounds like the guy you know?"

The young man became very serious. The smile he had worn from the time Kevin arrived vanished now.

"He can't be fired," the boy said.

"Why's that?"

"Who sent you to see me?"

"The guidance counselor at the high school."

"Mr. B? Okay, I know what he wants me to tell you about. Come on."

The boy motioned for Kevin to follow him, and he walked into an empty office. He flipped on the overhead light, pointed to a chair against the wall for Kevin, and pulled a second chair up so he was facing the reporter.

"Girardi arrested me once. If it had been any other cop, I would probably be in jail now instead of being a high school graduate holding down a job. It was a year or so ago, when CETA was still around."

"CETA? What is that?"

"The Comprehensive Employment and Training Act. It got jobs for kids who were in trouble. Anyways, I was having some trouble at home, and grass made it better. My grades got fucked up. I lost some friends and made some new ones. The new ones weren't good for me, but I didn't know it. So, I was sitting in the courtyard up against the building, and I guess I lost track of where I was, or I just didn't care, and I fired up. Girardi saw me from his window and came outside. He quietly walked to where I sat and was standing right over me before I knew it."

"And you thought this was a good thing?" Kevin asked.

The young worker looked down at his hands clasped in front of himself and continued. "No one even saw him do it. He took the joint and snuffed it out. He ground it into the dirt until you couldn't tell what it was. He took me inside the building and to the men's room. He says, 'Give me the rest.' Then he put his hand out."

"And you just gave it to him?"

"Right, I still don't know why. The guy just has a way about him. You know, we trusted him. You gotta understand, he would come into a classroom of kids who did everything every day to hide what they were doing from everyone, and he would ask, 'How many of you smoke grass,' and half the class would raise their hands. Then he would tell us why it was a stupid idea."

"But you could have gone to jail."

"Right, and he could have just frisked me, but he didn't. He respects kids like that."

"So how much did you have?"

"Well, you know the saying, five'll get you ten? I could have done twenty years. I had a dime bag."

"Damn, but obviously you didn't go to jail."

"He flushed it all. Told me I was being an asshole. He said he knew what I needed."

"And what was it he said you needed?"

"A job. Some responsibility. A couple days later, he came and found me and told me I had a job with CETA, and if I didn't go to the job, he would put me in jail. I finished school that year, and I've been working here ever since, even though CETA got shit-canned for corruption. Girardi is a good guy. I guarantee those kids are wrong about what he said."

"Are you still..."

"Smoking dope? Hell no. I promised him I wouldn't."

"Thanks for talking with me," Kevin said as he stood to leave. "This will help."

He found the others on the list, and they all had

similar stories. In each instance, Girardi was depicted as a bit unorthodox but honest and caring. By the end of the day, Kevin was convinced that the girls must have been mistaken. His column that weekend began, "When it comes to our kids, we would all like to believe everything is either black or it is white, but sadly it is mostly gray, and sometimes the gray area overshadows the truth of their situation."

The parents read the column. The girls, without prodding, came forward at the school with their parents, and Girardi kept his job. When he called to thank the hometown reporter, Kevin told him, "I'm happy it turned out the way it did, but you know, you might want to discard the word 'slut' from your vocabulary."

"Will do," the police officer agreed.

Not everything was as easily clarified.

CHAPTER FIVE
Friends and Enemies

The phone rang on Kevin's desk just as he had shut down his computer, grabbed his sport coat, and headed for the door. He stopped and looked at the phone, as if his stare would make it stop ringing. When it didn't, he stood stock still.

"What the hell are you doing?" Stanley asked from the desk next to Kevin's. The assistant managing editor, Pete, just smiled. "Approach/approach conflict," he said. He and Kevin had attended State College together and took the same psychology class. Pete also had a love of printer's ink and the truth. He had taken the first job he could get in the newspaper, in the layout room, and worked his way up to number three in the newsroom.

"Answer the damn phone," Weise, the editor, shouted. He couldn't think with that incessant ringing.

That made up Kevin's mind.

"Hello."

"Is this Kevin O'Connor?"

"Yes."

"This is Phil Lardner. I own the—"

"I know who you are, Phil. I went to school with your brother. What can I do for you?"

Phil Lardner owned a large construction company. He had graduated high school only a few years behind Kevin, and the afternoon after his graduation had a job driving a backhoe. Now he owned several behemoth machines.

Kevin sat down again at his desk, accepting the fact that he wasn't going to get to leave work early now.

"I rent a space in the Windenmere building."

"That's nice," Kevin said.

"Hey, don't be a wise ass. I've got something you might want to write about."

"Sorry, I was just about to… never mind. What can I do for you?"

"They're going to burn the building down."

"What building? Who?"

"The Windenmere building. Aren't you listening?"

"I thought that was empty."

"Most of it is. I rent a small part, and I think there are a few other people renting offices, but most of it is empty, and it's ready to burn."

"How do you know this?"

"Come visit me, and I'll show you."

"Okay. When?"

"Now would be good. I was told that if this building goes up, it could take out half the town."

"Right. See you in about…" Kevin checked his watch. "In about a half hour."

Kevin pushed his chair back, picked up his camera, and headed for the parking lot.

It was a short drive to Faithville, the town next to Halford. Kevin drove though the large, nearly deserted parking lot that had years ago been the employee's lot for nearly five hundred cars, but now had only two vehicles parked in lonely proximity to the end of the building.

He parked next to the Cadillac and walked in the end door of the expansive building.

He was met by a large, blond young man in steel-tipped black boots, dirty jeans, and a sweatshirt with the sleeves cut off.

"Come on," Lardner said, and strode off through the back of his office into the first floor of the empty building that used to be one of the largest manufacturing plants in the country. With all the machines gone, the room where Phil and Kevin now stood seemed spacious enough to house several small airplanes. The wooden floor was soaked with years of machine oil and chemical solvents. Clinging to the walls and ceiling was the smell of many decades of workers and their lunches, and of the peeling paint cascading like fluttering fingers from the ceiling. The only light was from the wall of dirty windows reaching from the top of the room to a point a handful of feet from the floor. The room was desolate, empty and quiet. The mill had left, picked up and moved south.

As they reached the end and were about to go through the huge metal fire doors into the next room, Phil turned to Kevin.

"Notice anything?" he asked, looking around himself and waiting for Kevin to get the hint.

"No, what?"

"We're standing between the rooms."

"Right, so?"

"We are standing where the fire doors should be. Why are they open?"

"Maybe they just forgot."

"No. They were closed a few days ago. Someone opened them recently. Come on."

Phil Lardner led the way, pointing out in every room that the fire doors were open. In each space, he stood in the opening and extended his arms, palms up, as if he had just finished performing a magic trick. Then he stepped through into a room even larger than the others, walked toward the middle and stopped next to a fifty-five-gallon drum. "Look at this," he said, pointing into the barrel.

Kevin looked. The barrel was stuffed with oil-soaked rags and newspapers.

He took out his camera and took a picture. Then he walked back and took pictures of the opened fire doors.

As they walked on, he also took pictures of the oil-soaked floors, the piles of loose debris, the broken windows letting in streams of air from outside, and the inch-wide, three-foot long strips of white, lead-based paint that hung from the ceilings of some of the rooms.

Every fire door was open and most of the windows were broken, allowing fresh oxygen to pour in from the outside.

When he had finished getting all the pictures his camera would allow, Kevin thanked Lardner and went directly to the fire barn to report the problem. He was told that the fire department could not just walk into a privately owned business.

"Well, you better do something, because, whether or not it is being done on purpose, it doesn't look good. It looks dangerous. By the way, how bad would it be if that building went up in flames?"

"Bad," the fire chief said. "It might take out most of the downtown."

Kevin returned to work and began writing his story.

The day after the story ran with the pictures, a small fire ignited a few feet inside one of the doors. The fire department was called, and after they put it out, it only stood to reason that they should check out the rest of the building. The fire department made the building as fire safe as it could be and left.

The next day, Kevin was threatened by an official in the town with the possibility of arrest for trespassing on private property.

"That's what you're worried about? Trespassing? I'll take that to court," Kevin said and hung up his desk phone. He heard nothing else about it. No harm, no foul.

After the fallout subsided, Kevin heard of how one of

the young women who worked overseeing some of the finances of the town had found discrepancies. He went to ask her about it.

"The chief took the cruiser on vacation with his family," she said.

"That ain't so bad, is it?"

"Not by itself but look here." She pointed at a line item, a very expensive subzero winter coat. "That's kind of expensive, and look here." She pointed at another line. "It appears as if much of his family vacation was charged on the town debit card."

After talking to the chief, who said it was "all bull shit," Kevin wrote the story, including both sides, the documentation, and the chief's assessment that it was "all bull shit." He quoted the chief as saying, "A policeman is always on duty." The chief also pointed out that "traffic duty gets cold," and that he had paid back the money on the card.

Townspeople began calling in to the newspaper with more and more accusations, some true, some exaggerated, some outright wrong. It seemed, according to at least one source, that the chief had been bringing cruisers to an autobody shop even when there didn't seem to be anything wrong with them and then adding the bill to his budget. "He's getting a kickback," was the accusation.

Kevin checked out the autobody shop, but there didn't seem to be any proof that this was happening. The work had been done and an appropriate amount had been charged, leaving no room for a kickback.

"DDC," Weise said to Kevin while they were both pouring coffee in the break room.

"What?"

"DDC," Weise repeated. "Dem Damn Cops."

"I don't know what that means," Kevin said, stirring the coffee with his finger as Weise poured Hennessey from a pint bottle into his coffee. "Want some?"

"No, thanks," Kevin answered, covering the cup with his palm. Weise continued, "Dem Damn Cops. Remember that most people don't like cops."

"Why's that?"

"Because most of the time when you see them, you're getting a ticket. In a blue moon, they are saving you or protecting you, but that happens like once in a lifetime. Most of the time it's the ticket, or you're getting arrested. So, most people don't like cops. They'll make a lot of stuff up about cops, and the problem is they might even believe their own lies. When you're writing about cops, be sure to prove everything." Weise began to walk away but stopped and turned. "And priests," he said. "Be sure to prove everything you hear about priests. I don't know why people lie about priests, but they do. Prove everything." He walked back into the hall and headed for the newsroom.

Then a story came to Kevin from a police officer in the next town. It seemed a man had just gotten a job on a construction site in Oxford. Oxford was more than a few miles away from Halford, where the man lived. When the young man finished his first day on the job, he was asked by his new boss to give a coworker a ride home. Of course, he had said okay.

When reaching the border of Faithville, he was pulled over for having no brake lights. His passenger, who he had only met for the ride home, jumped from the car and ran for the woods.

Before the afternoon was done, the passenger had been arrested on an outstanding warrant, and the driver, who tried to explain to the chief of police that he didn't even know the guy who ran, was beaten nearly senseless.

Kevin wrote the story and, again, he was threatened.

The voice on the phone said, "You better watch what you write, asshole. I know all about you."

"Is this about the kid who got beat up?" Kevin asked

the voice on the phone.

"What goes around comes around. Stick to writing about Halford. It's better for your health."

Kevin hung up the phone. He looked across the room at Stanley the copy editor. "I think I just got my first physical threat for something I wrote," he said.

"Good for you," Stanley said. "Got mine about thirty years ago. You must be doing something right."

It didn't seem that right when Kevin and his wife attended a high school reunion for everyone who had graduated from Windenmere High School and was still alive.

While his wife was dancing with an old boyfriend, Kevin went outside for a cigarette.

Every human being in five towns had been on this outside porch at one time or another, leaning against this very railing and looking into those same dark woods. Pretty much every high school dance in five towns was held here. Every Friday night with friends was spent at this pond in various altered states.

"Never changes, does it?"

The voice came from a middle-aged man who had been standing silently next to Kevin. He had a familiar face. Kevin looked at him and realized he should know who it was, but he didn't.

"No, I guess it doesn't," Kevin said.

"Do you know who I am?" the man asked. Short and squat, he had large, meaty hands and was balding.

Kevin looked again. "Sorry."

"You know my little brother Gary."

It all came back to him. This was his childhood friend Gary's older brother. The one who went to jail.

"You remember me now, don't you?"

"I do," Kevin said. "How are you doing?"

"It's more how are you doing? And how you're going to be doing if you aren't more careful."

Kevin wasn't enjoying the conversation, so he began to step by the man to go back inside.

"Hold on," the man said and stepped in front of Kevin.

"A friend of mine wanted me to give you a message."

Kevin said nothing but stopped and looked into the rat-like eyes of his human blockade.

"You remember I went to jail, right?"

Kevin didn't speak.

"You remember what I went in for?"

Kevin still just stared.

"I took a shot at a cop, remember?

Now Kevin was done. "I remember. I remember you

missed, too. I'm not worried. Tell your friend I said hi." He pushed past the man and re-entered the reunion.

A few minutes later, he explained to his wife that things at work were beginning to head in a different direction.

"What are you talking about?" she had asked.

"It's getting a bit more serious."

"Oh," she said. She smiled and told him about the great time she had at the reunion.

On the ride home, Kevin realized that they were like a couple of trains chugging along on parallel tracks, and before they reached their suburban driveway, he knew eventually one of the tracks would veer off and head in a totally different direction. The kids were growing up, and Kevin hoped he and his wife could make it through to their graduations from high school. He also realized he may have to figure out who was threatening him.

Within a few weeks, he got an afternoon call from a police officer in one of the outlying towns who wanted to meet with him at a local coffee shop.

As Kevin stepped inside the coffee shop and looked around for the man, he saw a familiar face waving at him from a corner booth. It was Mr. Pavrini, who used to live down the street from Kevin. As he sat down, the elderly policeman handed Kevin a brown manila envelope that was taped shut with clear mailing tape.

"I'm retiring in a month," he said. "I remember your family living up on the road out of town north. And I've been watching the things you write. I guess I trust you. Anyway, I need your help."

"Sure, Mr. Pavrini. What can I do for you?"

"Hold onto that envelope. It has some evidence in it about a murder a few years ago."

"What do you want me to do with it?"

"Just hold onto it, but if anyone comes after me when I retire, you go ahead and print it."

"I don't know if I can do that," Kevin said, fingering the envelope. "Do you mind if I take a look?" He started to open the envelope.

"Don't do that," the officer said. "As it is, it is just an envelope. If you open it, you would have to decide what to do with it. Just an envelope can go in a safe somewhere, like at the Beacon, okay?"

"Is this new evidence?" Kevin asked.

"No. It is all on the record."

"I'll run it by my boss," Kevin said.

The next day Kevin took it to his publisher who, after a phone call, agreed with the cop and put it in the company safe.

———

That afternoon, Kevin took pictures of the leaking generators at the nearly vacant Windenmere building. He was told by a state environmentalist that the stuff leaking had PCBs in it and could cause cancer. He wrote the story and was threatened by some out-of-town attorney.

"You don't want to end up in court over this," the attorney cautioned.

Kevin answered the voice on the other end of the line, "Hey, I'm just doing my job. I am supposed to write stories about the truth that I find. If your job is to take me to court for it, I guess you will have to take me to court. Hope I don't hear from you again," he said, and hung up.

The next day, the generators were removed.

Only a few weeks later, when he arrived at work, Weise told him, "There is an auction today. They're auctioning off the Windenmere building. I want you there."

Kevin took his camera and recorder and drove to the building. In front of the main door was a group of suits in expensive trench coats. Some in tan, some in black. Kevin thought it might be some kind of color-coded hierarchy, and started trying to figure out which were the bosses, which were the underlings.

He asked around and found that those in attendance were the board of selectmen, the finance board representative, the owner of the property, an auctioneer, and a bunch of lawyers.

"Who's bidding?" Kevin asked one of the selectmen.

"I don't know. I guess they aren't here yet."

Without much fanfare, the bidding began abruptly a few minutes later.

There was only one bid. The bid came in at about half of what the town said the building was worth on the tax rolls and it came from the current owner.

The bidding closed, and Kevin approached the town officials. They almost ran away, but he caught the chairman of the selectmen by the arm of his coat and asked, "Does he now pay half the taxes he paid this year?"

"I don't know. You'll have to ask the board of assessors." He hustled off to find the safety of his pack of trenchcoated friends.

Kevin wrote the story. Weise came to his desk. "Your column is too long. Cut it to fourteen inches. People these days are too busy to read any more than that. Either that or they're that stupid."

"But everything in there is fact. What do I cut?"

"You don't want the facts to get in the way of a good story," Weise said and began to walk back to his desk.

"I don't understand that," Kevin said.

Weise turned and sighed. Clearly, he wanted to be done. "You have a lot of facts in there."

"I thought that was a good thing," Kevin said.

"No," Weise said, pulling up a rolling chair from the vacant desk next to Kevin's.

"Everything you say is a fact in a story or a column must be a *provable* fact. It isn't good enough that you know it is a fact. You must be able to prove it. You understand that, right?"

"Right."

"So don't let the facts get in the way of a good story."

Kevin looked at Weise in the same way Kevin's dog used to look at him when he was being trained to sit. He cocked his head in abject emptiness.

Weise continued. "If you say in your column that Salk didn't take a penny for his polio vaccine, that's a fact. There are thousands of other facts about polio and Salk and vaccine, but that is the important one. Then you can say whatever you want about it. That's the opinion part. You can say he was a saint or a fool. If you go to court, the only thing you need to prove is the one fact. If you put in a hundred facts, you'll have to find things to be able to prove them for weeks, so?"

"Don't let the facts get in the way of a good story," Kevin said in total understanding.

He also understood that he was not making all that many friends with this job, but he was earning his keep by selling newspapers. He was doing his job by covering the things that mattered to the readership, what was important in their lives, and by telling the truth.

Before the fallout from the sale of the building subsided, the Catholic church in town came down. A new building was scheduled to replace it, and truckload by truckload the old building was demolished and disappeared.

One morning, nearly out of breath, Kevin entered the publisher's office.

"They're burying the Catholic church up on the hill," he said.

"Forget it," the publisher said with a smile.

"Forget it? That building is old."

"So what?"

"It has to be full of lead paint and asbestos."

"And?"

"And they are burying it uphill from the river."

"How do you know this?"

"I followed a truck this morning from the demolition up the hill and asked the guy driving the truck what he was doing. He said he was burying the asbestos shingles from the church. I told him it was illegal, and he said, 'asbestos is a mineral. It came from the ground, and I'm just putting it back where it belongs.' I got pictures." Surprisingly, the top gun at the paper put his hands flat down on his desk and looked directly into Kevin's eyes. "We are not going to take on the Catholic church," he said.

"Why not? Are you Catholic?"

"No, I'm not Catholic, but it's got nothing to do with religion."

"Then what?"

"Too much money. You want a job here, right? Well, we don't have to lose a libel suit to lose the paper. We could win and lose at the same time."

Kevin just sat without moving, so his boss continued, "This is how it happens. Someone with a bunch of money hires a brace of lawyers and sues, and even if everyone knows your story is accurate and true, it goes to court to make you prove it, and to prove you have no malice toward the plaintiff. Can you prove you have no malice toward the Catholic church? Then the paper is forced to hire lawyers. That costs money. The reporter, the editors, the publisher, and some other people from the paper or people hired by the paper's attorneys are all caught up in court for months, maybe years. The paper needs to hire more people to take the place of the ones who are constantly in court. Sooner or later, it becomes too expensive. The paper goes under, and the suit is dropped. You win, but you lose. In court, the guys with the deepest pockets win."

Kevin went back to his desk and began writing the story. He had the proof, the statement of the town worker, the pictures. Before he was finished, he was called into the office again.

"Kevin, I have just been told that if you are sued for what you write in your column, the owners are not going to back you up… no lawyers. You understand this, right? If you're sued, you'll be on your own."

He did understand. He could lose his house and everything else he owned. With one kid in college and one heading there, instead of writing the story, he turned his attention to the upcoming town meeting in Faithville.

Sitting in the break room of the newspaper, Kevin sipped coffee and smoked a cigarette while poring over the proposed budgets of the town. He had been asked to write a column about the town meeting. This was always a difficult assignment. Once a year, people got to talk about all the projects and budgets that would fill the pages of the paper for the next year. They liked to talk a lot, and Kevin had found there was never enough room in a reporter's note pad to write all his notes. Also, people had accents, or soft voices, or talked too fast, or referenced obscure things nobody ever heard of, and if you didn't know in advance the problems that were apt to arise, you were left in the dark writing everything down even if it wasn't important.

Suddenly he sat up, gathered the papers, and returned to his desk. He picked up the phone and called the young woman who oversaw the finances of the town.

"Is this line item right?" he asked. "The police budget has a line item of $2,000 for shotgun shells. Can that be right?"

"It's right. That's what he's asking for."

"How can that be right? Where the hell could the police department in Faithville have fired off $2,000 in shotgun shells?"

"I don't know. You'd have to ask him."

That night, Kevin attended the town meeting. About halfway through the discussion on the police department budget, a young father asked to be heard. He asked about the very thing that had confused Kevin.

"I think this $2,000 for bullets is pretty high," the young man said. "I think they are only about forty cents a shell."

As if summoned from the deep, the massive police chief appeared in the door at the back of the Town Hall auditorium. He walked halfway down the aisle and stared at the young father. He had one hand on the can of mace attached to his belt and one on his gun, and he stared at the speaker.

The speaker went on, "Well, I just think it is a bit much, that's all," he said and returned to his seat.

"Wait a minute," Kevin heard himself say as he stood up. He lived in the town. He had a right to get up and speak, so he did.

"Manny is right," he said with his eyes on the chief who stood in the center of the aisle. "That's a lot of shotgun shells."

The chief took a few steps forward.

Kevin turned to the moderator. "Are you going to let him do this?" he asked.

"Do what?"

"Intimidate people when they get up to say something about his budget?"

"He has a right to be here."

"Okay," Kevin said, turning back toward the chief who was now all the way to the front of the room, standing only a handful of feet away and glaring at Kevin.

"Okay." Kevin clenched the sides of the antique wooden podium, picked it up, and with one movement, turned it and slammed it down, facing the chief.

"Let's see if you intimidate me," he said, then to the townspeople at the meeting he asked, "How many of you have heard a shotgun go off in town this year? Raise your hand if you have." He never looked back at the people.

"No hands raised at all? Damn, the town is only five square miles, seems if a shotgun was fired, two thousand dollars' worth of shells, maybe what, four, five thousand shots, someone might have heard something. If you let this go through, try to remember this town also has about one square mile of water. Next year, he's going to want a boat."

Kevin shook his head at the chief, turned his back, and walked to his seat. The budget was adjusted, but now he had a full-fledged enemy who would like to have fired just one of those shells into Kevin's back as he walked to his seat, and all just for doing his job, telling the truth. That was not unexpected, but it was surprising to Kevin that there were other people in town who also felt the way the chief did.

"Are you insane?" his wife asked as he stepped inside the front door that night. "I watched it on TV. You have two teenage kids, so you pick a fight with the chief of police who has a habit of whacking teenagers in the head with his flashlight or arresting them for being suspicious looking people, kids walking the streets in their own hometown? Are you crazy?"

"It's my job," Kevin tried.

"It's your job? You stupid son of a bitch. You better get rid of him before he starts looking at them as punishment. Damn it, why couldn't you just sell office supplies?"

"I can't just get rid of him. He would have to get rid of himself. I'm just printing the truth of what he's doing. His job is up to the townspeople and the selectmen."

But before Kevin could get back to investigating the situation, something new happened.

The town of Halford was debating whether or not to build a Vietnam Memorial in the park in its center. It seemed it would be a done deal, but then someone came up with promises made at the time when the park had been built.

Kevin drove to the center of Halford, parked his car outside the police station, and walked to the park. It was a small park, no more than about fifty yards long and twenty-five yards wide, but it was pretty. It was surrounded by an arborvitae hedge that had been trimmed to just above Kevin's head when he was about ten years old. He used to play here after his family had moved into town. It encompassed a meticulous lawn. On one end stood the memorial to WWI and WWII, and there were benches on the other side. Smack in the middle was a huge metal statue of a man on a horse. The promise had been made to the metal man riding the bronze stallion.

The contention was that the Major would build a park for Halford as long as nothing else was built in it that would detract from his statue.

Kevin opened the folded papers he had carried with

him, sat on a bench, and began to read. The documents had been given to him by a state government official with the advice of, "Read this carefully. It's all in the semantics."

So, he did, and after having read several times the promise made many years before, it dawned on him what his benefactor had meant. He went to work and wrote the story.

"The promise made to the Major so many years ago must be kept," he said. "A promise is a promise.

"It doesn't matter that the major was instrumental in taking half of Halford's tax base with him when his town broke off and went its own way. A promise is a promise. It doesn't matter that there is a memorial there already. A promise is a promise, and the town of Halford promised it would not build 'another edifice' in the park. A promise is a promise, and there should not be another edifice built," Kevin wrote.

"But a Vietnam memorial that is not a building, not an edifice, would be okay. It wouldn't break any promise."

The memorial was built several months later. It was only a few feet high and looked more like a short wall than an edifice. It had engraved in it all the names of the soldiers from the town who had served in Vietnam. They surrounded the Major but didn't detract from the beauty of his horse that many of the townspeople said had its ass pointed toward Halford and was galloping toward Faithville.

Shortly after, the board of selectmen in Faithville decided that when the chief's contract was ended, it would be a good time to get a new chief.

CHAPTER SIX
When the Bullets Become Real

Covering the local small-town problems grew up into a whole different animal when Kevin O'Connor was sent to cover a city courtroom.

A trial that included assault and battery, gun wielding, payoffs, cops, and confidential informants, sent him to the paths around the lake near his old home to contemplate why it was still important to tell the truth when it could just as well be left in the dark and protect his kids.

Either way, he would still draw his paycheck, and his life might be simpler.

The day before the trial was to start, Kevin went to the lake that he had always found comforting. The lake was in the woods where he had fished when he was a boy. He sat on an old and rotted log at the water's edge. A translucent green firefly hovered in the sunshine, barely gripping the tip of a stock of grass, and looked at Kevin from a few feet away. The iridescent bug was one of the oldest beings on the planet. It flitted from flower to grass stalk in the sun-filled afternoon, and the high-pitched whine of the cicadas was a welcomed backdrop to his thoughts.

"Why the hell am I doing this?" Kevin thought. "My family doesn't want me to. People in the town don't want the complications, I'm being threatened from everywhere, my church probably even stopped me from telling the truth about them, and the people I work for won't back me up. Why is it so damn difficult to tell the truth? Why is the truth so important when no one wants to hear it?"

"They don't want to be informed," the dragon fly seemed to tell him. It left the grass shoot and flew closer to his face. "They just want to be entertained."

Kevin thought about this past handful of years.

It was a distinct possibility that he had helped build a memorial to a group of dead soldiers no one wanted to remember. He had brought to light seeming corruption and lawlessness by those who were supposed to be enforcing the laws, and then helped save a policeman's job because it was the right thing to do. He made people aware of the innocence of a kid who had been arrested for nothing, had pointed out cancer-causing chemicals leaking into the river, had illuminated a scheme to pay fewer taxes by a rich man, helped prevent a town-wide conflagration, helped put an end to traffic taxing in a small town, helped house a burned-out family, and explained the use of the daily police log.

"Damn," he told the dragonfly, who was now hovering around his head. "I have shown them the fraud, corruption, double-dealing, brutality, lawlessness, pollution, and lack of safety that exists right in the middle of their lives. I pointed out that some young people are doing good for their communities and helped add money to worthwhile fundraisers. And what do I get for it? I get threatened by lawyers and thugs. And the only thing they really like is the jokes, the sex, the outrageous. The story that people liked the most was the one about the black man who was looking for a job in Faithville, and when he was inevitably told no, he had headed for the center of town to use the phone booth, and within an eighth of a mile he was arrested for being "a suspicious looking person." In other words, he was arrested for being black in a white town.

Kevin had said it was pure racism, the same racism

that hid behind the red lines in the real estate corners of even a small Unitarian, New England hamlet. He pointed out that the racial hatred that had lain dormant, under rocks and behind trees in the "land of the free," was beginning to come out into the light again, but that isn't what readers had seen.

What he heard most from the folks in coffee shops that week was that they thought it was funny. That a man was arrested for the color of his skin made them laugh.

"This journalism thing isn't heading in a good direction as far as I can see," Kevin said out loud, and watched as the dragon fly flew into the woods and landed on an ancient, rusted yellow steamroller.

Kevin heard himself say, "What the hell is a steamroller doing in the middle of the woods?" Then he really thought about that question. What the hell was a steamroller doing in the middle of the woods?

He looked farther beyond the tree line and saw a flash of porcelain. Focused on these objects, Kevin followed the clues into the woods to the nearly overgrown path and found a stove, a bathroom sink, and a washing machine. A few yards down the path were black plastic bags of garbage, and some old metal buckets that had sat there long enough for the bottoms to have rotted out.

That night, before his next day trial coverage, he wrote a column asking the town of Halford why it was allowing the path beside his pristine lake to become so filthy. He asked why this path that ran by the cemetery, where his father's friends and the adults of his childhood were buried, was such an insult to the graves. A few months later, a good thing happened. The cleanup began, and the paving of the path and the metamorphosis of the walkway through the woods and around his lake became a real plan.

The trial was a different story.

On the first day of court, Kevin heard an eviction story. A young, unmarried couple had rented an apartment above a bar in a town just outside the city. The young woman was from Halford, so the Beacon, along with some larger newspapers, would be covering the story of them being beaten severely one night.

It seemed the owner of the bar wanted the young couple to move out. Eviction rules were beginning to favor the poor at the time, and it was becoming more and more difficult to toss a family out on its ass. The couple had paid their rent and kept the place clean, and they said they wouldn't leave. Some people were hired to take care of the situation, and two of them had broken in and beaten the couple as an incentive for them to move out. Now, those who allegedly had beaten them were on trial.

In the days to follow, somehow, testimony was beginning to hint that police officers had also been involved.

Kevin covered the trial by codifying the ongoings inside the courtroom, but also by interviewing the witnesses, the defendants, the police, and the confidential informants. His stories had enlarged the scope of the trial. People were beginning to pay attention. A week after the beginning of the trial, Kevin was hurrying to the elevator on the second floor of the city courthouse as fast as possible because his kids would be getting home soon. As the doors began to close, a man ran to the door calling, "Hold the elevator!"

Kevin stuck his foot in the doors to allow the guy to get on. The stocky man in the gray suit and close-cropped hair smiled at him, and as the door closed again, the man took a pistol out of his shoulder holster.

"You are going to watch what you write, aren't you?" The man's mouth twisted upward as he pointed the pistol toward Kevin's head.

The man didn't look all that intimidating to Kevin, but

the gun did. "What are you talking about?"

"This trial. Stop talking to the CI and stop saying police were involved. These two guys are going to jail. They did it. They belong in jail, and the two druggies belong on the street."

Kevin never found out who the man was, but as they approached the first floor, he said, "So, your brilliant idea is to shoot me in the courthouse elevator? What are you, insane? Get the fuck out of my way!" He pushed his way past the man into the open foyer, made a beeline past the row of telephone booths, and headed for the crowded street outside. Sitting in his car in the back parking lot, Kevin took the first breath he remembered taking since the gun had come out. He never saw the man or his gun again. He kept writing exactly the way he had been, and one of the men was found innocent. The involvement of police never surfaced in court. In the end, it all came down to which side had the better lawyers.

And speaking of lawyers, Kevin's divorce finally happened. He and his wife had managed to hang on until both their kids were in college. For two people who hadn't liked each other very much for the past twenty years, it had been a major achievement. The judge was impressed that the two had imposed on themselves the balancing of the financial burden. His daughter was on the verge of graduating, so her tuition was ending, and they split his son's tuition. The kids stayed on his health insurance. She paid for food and clothing. He paid for the upkeep of the kids' car. The house was sold and the money split. He refused to take any of her 401k, and she let the vacation timeshare slip away. In court, as the divorce was finalized, the judge congratulated them for a "sane divorce," an idea that didn't catch on in the town where they lived as everyone began taking sides and whispering lies.

Within a year, Kevin was remarried to a woman he was sure was his soul mate, and they began a life together, but as their new life started, something unexpected happened.

The publisher called Kevin in to the office one morning, about a week before Christmas, and told him. "The paper is being sold."

Not only was it being sold, but it was being combined with the paper that had been their major competition for decades, the one that had tried to bankrupt the Beacon. The one Kevin had bolted from when he was asked to help destroy the Halford paper.

The end was in sight.

Before the transfusion of city blood had finished transforming the Beacon into something nearly unidentifiable, Kevin got a close-up view of what journalism was becoming.

First, the long-time hierarchy of the Beacon was set adrift into the atmosphere with a partial parachute that wouldn't protect them as they fell to the ground. The top few in every department were let go and replaced with underlings from the city paper. The needs of the people of Halford and twelve other towns took a back seat to the needs of cutting the overhead costs of the Beacon so it could be resold.

The staff was thinned out and the press was sold off, and along with it the printer's ink. The printing plates were loaded every morning into the back seat of an automobile and shipped to the city to be printed on their presses.

At a morning meeting several weeks into the new arrangement, the newspaper, for the first time in a century, missed putting out a newspaper. There was a meeting to chastise those who were deemed to have been the cause.

The new editor stood at the head of the table and said

in ominous tones, "We need to do some work on our procedures to make sure this doesn't become prevalent. Reporters and photogs need to get their work in earlier, which may mean editors will need to be in earlier to clean up the stories. The camera room and plate room will need to get the layouts earlier. I understand you at the Beacon aren't used to getting things done on time. I know it has been a looser set of rules here in the past, but we can't have this happening again, so we will be changing all your starting times to avoid this problem. Are there any questions?" He scanned the room. "Yes, Mr. O'Connor."

"Have you actually checked to see what caused the problem, or are you just assuming stuff?" Kevin asked.

"Yes. The plates didn't get to the press on time. I thought that was obvious."

"So, you're going to have everyone come in earlier, in the middle of the night, to remedy this?"

"Do you have a problem with that, Kevin?"

"Well, since the plates got into the car earlier than usual and still didn't get to the press on time, I assumed you knew that you were basing the success of your operation, your tighter set of rules, on a twenty-five-year-old single mother with a three-year-old boy and a one-year-old girl in a seven-year-old Hyundai that broke down on the way to the press, and she had to get someone to come pick up her kids who were in the back seat at the time before she continued on to get the plates to the press. That could be the reason. Did you think of that?"

"I didn't know that is what happened. I was…"

"How about this," Kevin broke back in. "Instead of tearing up the lives of what—thirty people?—you just give the woman a raise so she can buy a better car. Or for that matter, wouldn't it be better if you just bought her a better car? I mean, if you really wanted to remedy this problem instead of encouraging us all to quit, but then you don't have to pay as many people when you fire us. That's what you're doing, right?"

"We'll consider what you have said."

The next week, the new schedules began.

Within a few months, the wholesale downsizing began, and the Halford Beacon died.

Thousands of people called in to cancel their subscriptions.

The name remained, but, with the new out-of-town staff, the loyalty that had been felt to the local people became just something that used to be. Halford became under-covered, and the other surrounding towns became totally ignored. People who had spent their lives producing local journalism for the people of the Halford area were summarily fired and scrambled to get jobs at Staples, McDonalds, schools, and grocery stores. They were replaced with those from the city newspaper who had no institutional knowledge of the local area, and with the watchdog aspect of local journalism being washed out the door, the Halford Beacon and thousands of local newspapers going through the same turnover, became, for all intents and purposes, advertisers with a few meaningless stories in them to retain at least some of the readership.

Reporting on local corruption became too costly. Fraudulently padding town budgets went unnoticed. The PCBs from the generators in abandoned factories leaked their way into the drinking water of small towns. The jobs of teachers and cops teetered on the edge of the whims and fancies of ill-motivated townspeople with fabricated torches and pitchforks, and no one came to help. Local journalism welcomed the saleable commodity of sensationalism, mistakes, and outright lies. Don't let the facts get in the way of a good story became the following mantra: forget about the facts completely. Lie if you must, as long as it boosts readership and sells advertising.

CHAPTER SEVEN
The Valiant Losing Fight

Kevin took a job in New Hampshire, and he and his new wife, Vivian, moved north to Laconia, the home of Lake Winnipesaukee, the Fighting Football Sachems and Bike Week.

During his first year in the Lakes Region, 350,000 motorcycles came to the small city of 14,000 people. It was fun, exciting. Drinking tents went up, and booths sold t-shirts that said, "If You Can Read This, The Bitch Fell Off" or "Fuckin' Donuts" popped up along the roadsides.

Kevin's plea to curb the crass nature of the celebration of motorcycles at the same time as high school graduation was not accepted as desirable. The decadent week made too much money for prominent citizens for them to want any changes. Neither was his question about not wearing motorcycle helmets accepted, and he didn't become anyone's buddy for reminding the biker groups that "human heads don't bounce."

But he didn't get any death threats until he wrote about the full-page, four-color ad in the paper that the state bought to sell liquor on Fathers' Day at a cut rate. He guessed daddies needed cheap booze, and the state could make a lot of money selling it to them. It seemed getting shit-faced drunk was considered one of New Hampshire's constitutional rights.

One morning over coffee at a pre-work coffee shop, a patron asked Kevin, "So, do you ski?"

"No. I used to, but I stopped after high school."

"Do you drink?"

"No, I gave it up."

"If you don't ski and you don't drink, what the fuck are you doing here?"

That week, an underage girl was arrested while stripping at one of the clubs. Some townspeople were upset that she was drinking. No one seemed all that upset that the sixteen-year-old was stripping naked at the time in front of a bunch of old men.

Kevin's column made a modest proposal as his way of asking if there was perhaps too much drinking going on in the city. He asked if the state wasn't short-changing women, and he proposed there should be a sale on alcohol on Mothers' Day too, and perhaps the sign at the border with Massachusetts could be changed to say, "Welcome To New Hampshire. Would You Womens Like Some Licker?"

As he had hoped, people began hating him, but they picked up the paper every day just so their anger could be fed, and the paper grew.

The men who had put the money into building the new newspaper put continual pressure on Kevin to publish more sensational stories, but Kevin kept telling them that was the business plan of the newspaper down the street, the one that was their direct competition.

He sat at a meeting with the owners, who wanted to fire him, and the publisher, who half-heartedly supported him. The publisher knew his paper was growing, but he didn't know why. The two people who had put up the money for the paper wanted "more enterprise stories."

Enterprise stories meant stories that a reporter goes out and finds without having it handed to him or her at a government meeting or in a press release.

Kevin sat at the long conference table and waited while people shuffled papers around. Finally, he took the initiative to begin the meeting.

"I took some time last week and read the last six months of your newspaper up north, and the first six months of our paper," Kevin said to them. "And then I read the first six months of your paper when you first started it. Our newspaper here in the south had twice as many enterprise stories as yours had in the past six months, and three times as many as you had in the first six months of your newspaper. So, I don't think we are talking about the same thing when we say enterprise stories. Maybe you should explain what you mean."

"We mean stories that scream at you," he was told. It was decided that enterprise meant stories about rapes, murders, corruption… all the fun stuff.

"Or stories about people who kill pets? You mean sensational stories," Kevin said. "We shouldn't do that."

"Why not?"

"That's what everyone is doing. If we try to sell the same thing people are already getting from other newspapers, why would they pick up ours? We need to provide a local newspaper that protects them, that helps them, that supports them. It needs to be a paper that tells them what went on while they were working that day."

"But they buy sensational stories in our paper, and we are doing just fine," the editor of the northern paper said.

"You started your paper with no competition, right? There was no other newspaper in town, right? If you are the only game in town, people tend to play that game. Now, we have competition. In your case, they pick up the paper because there is no other paper. In our case, we need to make them pick it up but then realize it is a good paper."

Kevin waited a beat to assess whether he was getting his point across. "They will buy sensationalism at first, but they won't continue to," he said. "After a while, they'll get tired of it. They will start complaining about it, and they will eventually just shit-can newspapers altogether. Trust me. If we build a solid base with rational, informative, and helpful facts, they will eventually get our paper, and the other paper will close its doors."

"You think you can put the other paper under? It's a hundred years old." The money men laughed out loud.

"No. We won't put them under, but the people who live here will."

Kevin's new wife, Vivian, had a knack for finding meaningful feature stories that people wanted to read.

Between her full-time job in a chiropractor's office and her full-time schoolwork, she took the time to sell ads and write stories. She interviewed a biker who rode around with a wolf as his passenger. She asked him how long he had been out of his mind. He laughed and told her. She interviewed Kevin Spacey when he came to visit. He talked to her on the phone for an hour. She also did a story about the local prison. A former prisoner told her he had gotten a degree while in prison and then, when he got out, he had gotten a loan and started his own restaurant. She asked him why everyone shouldn't go to prison if they can get a free education and money to start a business. He told her that when he had been freed, he had a difficult time whenever he got to a closed door. He said he had always waited for a few seconds for someone else to open it. "Because for many years, every door in my life had been locked, and someone else had the key. Believe me," he told her, "It isn't worth it."

People picked up the paper to see what sensational, off-the-wall idea Kevin's column spoke of that day, but then read the rest of the paper, which was filled with well-thought-out, well-researched, well-written articles that helped the people who read them. The publisher wrote political stories, the new reporter covered town government, Kevin covered local sports and wrote his column, and Vivian did in-depth features about the people of the area.

The paper became popular for all of it.

Fourteen hours a day, six or seven days a week, Kevin wrote, took pictures, assigned stories, edited, and laid out the newspaper. When he felt he needed a break, he hired a photographer who took better pictures than he did. He covered planning boards, selectmen, school boards, local sports, police, fire, and even the Bike Week committee.

Sometimes on Sundays, he and Vivian would enjoy the mountain paths of Red Hill or the lakeside beach, but mostly they worked.

Then, shortly after Bike Week left town in the second year of his tenure in the city, Kevin found something that shocked him.

He wrote about it.

"Every single man or woman who was elected to any position in this city should be ashamed of him or herself. How dare you?" he wrote. "The city lost money on Bike Week? Are you kidding me?"

The city had gone, astonishingly, into debt promoting, producing, housing and cleaning up after the week of celebration when hundreds of thousands of people came to play and spend money.

Kevin wrote, "How can a city lose money when 350,000 motorcycles, with at least one person on every seat, arrived with two pockets full of money and the willingness to spend it all in one week?"

The city had been undercharging for each tent or table that was put up on city land. Every other parking lot in town was making money, but the city was charging sixteen dollars a spot for people to sit and sell t-shirts, bike parts, trinkets, and other paraphernalia, and when the cleanup was done, and the extra police hours were paid for, and the fireworks and everything else was paid for, the city lost money. But everyone else was getting rich.

Kevin pointed out the next day something he had been told by one of the Motorcycle Club members. This person was picking up copies of the paper because of Sonny Barger's picture on the front page; Sonny was the outlaw biker who was a founding member of Hell's Angels. The man glanced at the picture, then up at Kevin, then said, "Hey, did you know the banks spent the entire day making out bank checks for $599 to be sent out of state?"

Kevin had been watching him and wondering if he

knew Sonny. "Why $599?" Kevin asked.

"Because the bank has to report anything $600 and up, and people would get taxed on it." The young biker laughed and offered to pay for the papers.

"It's a free paper. I'm not going to take your money," Kevin said.

The young man shook his head. "And you're laughing at the city for undercharging?"

"You think that's funny," Kevin added. "It's a free paper. We drop off fifty or seventy-five papers at each stop at the coffee shops and the convenience stores, and we have a bunch of boxes around the city where we drop off a handful. Last week, I asked why we don't raise our rates on advertising, and I was told that the circulation number isn't high enough."

He waited and within seconds the young man asked, "Who decides how many papers you drop off in each place?"

"We do," Kevin said.

"So, why the fuck don't you just drop off more? Wouldn't that mean the circulation was up?"

"I'm not in charge," Kevin said, and they both laughed.

As the biker got to the door, Kevin called out to him.

"Did you hear about the one where a father had owned

a newspaper and then handed it over to his son?"

"No," the young man said, and he turned back to hear the story.

"So, one day the son brings the father back into the newspaper and shows him the new shit he has added. He says, 'Dad, it's a new world, and last month we caught up to it. We went online.'

The father asks, 'Online? What's that?'

'Well, we have our paper on the internet. People can get it on their computers at home.'

'How much does that cost them? the father asks.'

'Nothing. It's free, the son says, smiling.'

So, the father stopped walking and turned to his son. 'What fucking brilliant son of a bitch decided to give the newspaper away for free?'

'It was a good idea,' the son said.

'How do you figure that?'

'Our circulation went up from 20,000 to 35,000.'

Now the father got real serious. 'With a printed newspaper, it has always been the rule that for every person who buys a paper, five other people read it. You know, wife, husband, kids, five others. This online bullshit, only one person reads each, what did you call it, each hit? So, we were selling the paper for thirty-five cents to

20,000 readers, and then we were charging for the ads at the circulation number of 120,000. Now you give it away, and your circulation number is 35,000. Good job asshole.'

The son didn't answer."

"See ya. Have a good day." The young biker smiled and left.

Sometime during the second September at the paper, Kevin heard of a problem with the mascot of the high school football team.

A young man had walked into the front room of the newspaper carrying a tomahawk.

Kevin noticed it because the reporter who had been working in the outer office suddenly appeared in Kevin's office and leaned back against the wall so he would be out of sight of the person who had just walked in.

"Something I should know?" Kevin asked without looking up from the layout of page four.

"There's a guy here with a hatchet."

Kevin pushed his rolling chair away from his computer and leaned back so he could see the outer office. To his surprise there was, in fact, a young man with a hatchet looking back at him and grinning.

Kevin got to his feet and walked out to greet the visitor.

"Is there some problem we have?" he asked.

"The sachem is the holy man," said the visitor.

"That's nice," said Kevin. "Anything else?"

"Well, the mascot of the local football team is the sachem."

"Okay, so why are you in my office with a weapon?"

"Because I wanted to get your attention. There are a lot of Native Americans living here, and this warpath warrior calling himself a sachem is cheering like a maniac on the sidelines of the high school football games."

"Well," Kevin said, "that is pretty degrading, but what do you want me to do about it?"

"Write about it. Do what you do. Tell them the truth about what they are doing. It's really insulting."

"Are you an American Indian?" Kevin asked.

"No."

"Then what is your stake in it?"

"I just think it's wrong."

Kevin agreed he would investigate it, and the young white man with the hatchet left the building.

Kevin went to a game, witnessed the man dressed as

a Plains Indian warrior. He watched horrified as this cartoon character kept running up and down in front of the high school fans and their parents calling himself the sachem, waving his hatchet, and shouting how the Sachems should "scalp" the other team.

It was just plain wrong.

After Kevin's column that weekend, a young mother at the next school committee meeting wept and stood in front of the board and pleaded.

"You don't understand," she said. "I am a Sachem. My mother was a Sachem. My father was a Sachem, and his father was a Sachem. And now my children are Sachems. We can't let them make us change our identity for some damn politically correct bull-crap."

After the cheering stopped, she was followed by a young American Indian who lived in town.

He stood silently for a few seconds, then looking directly at the young woman. He began softly. "Respectfully," he said. "Respectfully," he repeated. "I live here too. I went to the school here too. I never said anything until now, but I was asked to come here and speak. You are not a sachem, and although I know your father to be a good man, he is not a sachem, neither is your mother. A sachem is the holy man of an American Indian tribe. What you do is insulting to us. It always has been. But we always knew you didn't mean it to be. I think it might be time, now that you know, to change it."

A man shouted from the audience. "Bull. This school has always been the sachems. We aren't going to change it."

"What you do is not up to me. It is up to you. I was just asked to let you know that it is insulting to my people." He nodded to the young mother and took his seat.

The anger intensified. Rats were stuffed inside the front door of an American Indian store in town, young men urinated at the entryway to the home of another Native American, and finally some of the indigenous people were forced to move out of town.

The only holdout was the newspaper and Kevin's column.

But the half-life of a newspaper story is usually halfway to the next good story. Most often that is a few days or so. The Sachem mascot prevailed, and the beginning of "might is right" replacing "common sense" was obvious. Self-righteous hardness replaced empathy. It was a precursor to the false outrage that would eventually become the way of life in the country.

Soon, Kevin was explaining to the people in the

adjacent town that building a new and bigger school would cost much more than the original cost of the building itself. There would then be more teachers to pay, higher heating costs, higher air conditioning costs, higher electric and water bills, and the increased cost would go on every year.

He also tried, on the very next weekend, to explain that in an outdoor entertainment venue where all the senior citizens and children living for miles around could hear the music being played over loudspeakers and the words being sung, it might not be a great idea to bring in Eminem to visit on a Saturday night. They didn't listen until he started singing.

His next column pointed out several ways the city could make money on Bike Week, including selling to those who were arrested, a framed mug shot with the words "Busted at Bike Week" across the bottom, or providing pay toilets for the beer tents at no charge to the people selling the beer, the proceeds going directly to the city.

At one point, his column brought in complaints from a rabbi and a Palestinian businessman on the same day about the same column. They both complained that the column had favored the other in Kevin's assessment of the problems in the Middle East.

He called them both and offered to sit down with them. He made their appointments at the same time and place. When they arrived in his office, he said, "Now, before you both get to do what I have brought you here to do, let me say this. When you stop lobbing rockets into residential areas in Jerusalem, and when you stop machine gunning kids for throwing rocks, and when you both stop blaming God for your practice of killing each other for stupid reasons, I will give you both a real time and place to air your grievances, but since you both think the exact same column was biased toward the other side, let me say this. The problem isn't with the column. It is with you two. The column espouses the benefit of freedom of the press, freedom of speech, and freedom of religion, while providing a check on those who make the rules and wage the wars. You both think I was supporting the other side. I feel you are wrong. I feel that you are paranoid. I have a lot of work to do. Get the hell out of my office."

Two years after Kevin had stepped into the empty office of what would become the newspaper with the publisher and made a list of what furniture they would need, he was called into the publisher's office.

"Kevin, you know how I told you that when we broke even, I would raise your pay to the going rate for the editor of daily paper? Well, we just broke even. We can now pay all the bills and make money."

"Great, but I can tell by your face you aren't about to give me a raise."

"No. I personally have run out of money in the process, so I need your paycheck myself so I can pay my mortgage. Soon we will be making money, but not yet. I'm going to have to let you go. You did a great job. The paper can now run without you."

"Don't worry," Kevin said. "I always win. I will win this time."

Within weeks, Kevin had a job as the wire editor of a large city newspaper in Connecticut and was offered the going amount of money that would have been expected had the Laconia paper paid what it had promised.

Kevin and Vivian took a break from packing for the move to Connecticut and took a short ride to the park down the street. It occurred to Vivian that they still lived in a place where you could have pizza delivered to the town park, so she dialed the local pizza place on her new cell phone and did exactly that.

"What do you think?" he asked his wife.

"About what?"

"About newspapers. You think they're done?"

She rolled over and sat up, looking at the backdrop of Lake Winnipesaukee. "The local ones are. I think the city papers will go on for a while. I guess the big question is, will that be okay."

The pizza arrived, and the young boy who had brought it now stood over the blanket where his two customers sat. As Kevin paid him, he looked up at the boy who was maybe eighteen years old and asked, "What would you think if the newspapers in town went under?"

"What do you mean?" the boy asked.

"If they both just went belly up, and there were no more newspapers to buy in Laconia."

"I could care less. I don't read the newspaper."

Kevin held onto the money a few seconds longer.

"Couldn't. You couldn't care less. Why not? Where would you find out what is going on?"

"Like what?"

"Never mind," Kevin said.

"Give the kid his money," Vivian said with a laugh.

They watched as the delivery boy walked back to his

car, not seeming to have a care in the world.

"It's a good question," Kevin said.

"What is?" Vivian answered while eating her dinner.

"Like what? It's a good question. What if local papers went under? I've been on local papers for about eighteen or twenty years. You've been doing it longer, and what have we done for the towns we wrote about? I mean, what will they miss?"

"Let's figure it out. What have you written about in those small towns?"

Kevin got up from the blanket and sat on one of the lawn chairs they had brought with them. He reached for a second piece of pizza.

"Corporations polluting the town, killing trees and flowers and berries."

"What?"

"It was the first story I wrote about. I wasn't even working for a paper at the time, but there was a paper I could get it printed in."

"You wrote about that fire in Halford," Vivian said.

"Right. I got that family a place to stay. And I wrote about corruption in town government. How are people going to vote if they don't know anything about the people they are voting for?"

Kevin continued, "Then there was religion versus politics in Faithville, and military versus protestors in Halford."

He had another bite.

"I did some free advertising for town craft fairs. They're going to miss that. And I gave kudos to some young people who were unselfish and helping their towns. And fundraisers, you know, helping advertise by writing a column about them."

"Didn't you write a local hero's column in that city paper you wrote for?"

"I did, and then there are the police logs so you know where your kid is if he gets arrested, and court cases. I did a lot with police, pros and cons, and the dangers in small towns where greed replaces safety. And tax fraud and misappropriation of town funds." He thought for a few more bites. "Then there was the story about protecting the innocent when they are wrongfully arrested."

"You helped get that Vietnam veterans' memorial in Halford."

"Right, even though my name isn't on it."

"Why not?"

"I went in from Faithville. I helped local towns remember their past, questioned the utility of some of their laws that were outdated."

"I guess that answers the question of whether or not local newspapers will be missed," Vivian said.

"But what about the question of why they couldn't care less?"

"I guess they aren't going to miss them until they do, until people who are voting will be choosing their heroes by listening to the loudest jerk at the coffee shop."

They cleaned up the remnants of napkins and crusts and tossed them into the pizza box and drove back to the house to finish packing for the move to the city paper.

CHAPTER EIGHT
The Beginning of the End

———————

They had been lied to, and he had been told it wasn't personal, just business.

It was the same thing that newspapers were telling their readership. *We are no longer telling you the whole truth, but don't worry. It's just business, nothing personal.*

Kevin and Vivian sold their condo in New Hampshire, drove south, and moved to a hotel in Shelton, Connecticut. He went to work at the city newspaper, and she took a job as a massage therapist. They spent the time they had after working to search for a home.

Vivian soon left her job and set up her new clinical massage therapy business. It grew on the strength of doctor referrals from the local hospitals, and within the year she had hired nine massage therapists to work at her four locations.

They bought a three-story house outside the city, and before they knew it, Vivian's parents were the victim of some predatory mortgage people and lost their home. The next day, they moved in with Kevin and Vivian.

Kevin threw himself into his work on the outwardly successful city newspaper. The daily circulation was over 100,000. His job was to decide which national and international stories would go into the paper every day, and on Sundays he got to give his opinion about them.

In 2006, Abu Masr Alzaqari, an Iraqi terrorist leader, was killed, and the Israeli/Hezbollah war raged.

He wrote about terrorism:

"The problem with terrorists is they have families, and when you kill one terrorist, you create an entire family of terrorists. And the circle never ends. There must be a better way."

In 2007, President Bush called for more troops to go to Iraq. He wrote about war crimes:

"If you haven't been to war, you don't get to say what is

and what is not a war crime. For instance, if you are in a war zone and you see a woman and a child walking down the path toward you and the boy stumbles and falls down on all fours, what do you do? If you didn't say immediately shoot the woman, you are dead. In Vietnam we learned this, because the boy would have a machine gun strapped to his back and the woman would open fire. If you haven't been to war, you would be quick to call shooting the woman a war crime. You would be wrong. War is hell. It is not a euphemism. It is hell."

In 2008, the country was arguing about the bank bailouts and the great recession.

He wrote about the redistribution of wealth:

"I'm not stupid. If Obama can't turn this around, and this country goes where it seems to be headed, it is going to be tough. But if you have had that singular American privilege of being brought up poor in a rich country, bring it on. We'll survive and let me tell you something. The rich were never really worried about a redistribution of wealth. They were worried about a redistribution of poverty.

Me?

I was just happy it trickled up to those who caused the problem in the first place."

In 2008, Obama used the internet to win the presidency.

He wrote about the addiction to technology:

"See him standing on a street corner smiling — black chinos, white shirt, collar up — a young man holding a small, red, plastic transistor radio to his ear and inhaling a toke from a friend's Jefferson Airplane, and the addiction starts.

They were right.

It led to harder things.

It led to the addiction we never talk about.

From that seemingly harmless mid-60s scenario grew a dangerous habit that is crippling the country.

No, it isn't shot into veins. It is pumped as loudly as possible directly into the brain for the same reason speed freaks and meth monsters do dope. It is to force out all other thoughts so a user can sit in irresponsible bliss for the duration of the high.

But this high never ends.

This generation is inundated with the woofer-heavy car radio, MP3, iPod, iPhone, Twitter, Facebook, Google, MySpace, Blackberries, laptops, Netflix, CDs, DVDs, huge-screen TV, video games, Game Boys, Xboxes, PlayStations, bluetooth, cellphones, visor-speakers, car TVs.

They are never unplugged, never off the wire.

With the proliferation and availability of the new technology, everyone can have it at some level.

And there is an observable and adverse outcome in this generation who pumps noise and visions so constantly into their heads that the brain has no time for its own creative thought.

Now, I know young people, and not all of them abuse this drug, and the ones who don't are ahead of where we were at their age.

But they are in an extreme minority.

Now, statistics show only about thirteen percent of Americans ages seventeen to twenty-four can even make it into the United States Army.

I think back to the advice my high school guidance counselor had for me in my senior year. He said, "With your lousy grades and worse attitude, your best bet is the Army."

And even I was put in Military Intelligence. We called it an oxymoron.

It's a different story now. Think about it.

Only twenty-four percent of those aged seventeen to twenty-four are even eligible to join the armed services. The biggest problem is obesity, and the second biggest is drug addiction.

Of those who are eligible and do apply, statistics say only about fifty-seven percent pass the intelligence test.

I have to say it. The test is not all that difficult.

So, eighty-seven percent of those between seventeen and twenty-four are some combination of fat, addicted, and stupid.

Why?

Because too many of them spend too much of their lives wired to technology, stuffing fast food, and sitting on their fat couches, doing drugs.

Technology can do a lot of good, but then again, so can drugs if used the way they were meant to be used.

The adverse effects of too much technology are more similar to the adverse effects of heroin than we want to believe, ending in wasted, unhealthy, and unproductive lives.

I'm sure some will disagree with this.

They will be outraged that I would say anything bad about their kids, risking the possibility that they might read it and have it lower their self-esteem.

I have three things to say about that.

First, given the high school dropout rate, your kids probably can't read. Second, sometimes having low self-esteem is just being a good judge of character, and third, no one can deny there's a problem when this generation has made the United States Army the intellectual elite of the country.

In 2008, the country was reeling from rising food prices, and some TV networks replaced news with entertainment that pretended to be news.

He wrote about war and homelessness:

"In Afghanistan, the Taliban sentences to death those who don't believe in their religion.

In Iran, those voicing opinions in the streets are beaten or killed by government thugs.

In China, the Internet is censored because people use it to criticize the government.

And last year outside our borders, sixty journalists were killed, 673 arrested, 929 were physically attacked or threatened, 353 media outlets were censored, and 29 journalists were kidnapped.

But in America, we enjoy our freedoms of religion, speech, press and assembly.

And in America, on any given night, between 154,000 and 200,000 men and women who took up arms and defended those freedoms of religion, speech, press and assembly are living in the alleys, dumpsters and doorways of the nation — hungry, sick, cold and defeated.

Over the course of a year, the number comes embarrassingly close to a million veterans who are homeless at one time or another.

And we let it happen.

It doesn't even seem to bother us. Well, not the way "really important things" bother us.

It isn't new.

It has happened after every war. When those who stand on the wall and fight get back from war, we have a unique way of handling them.

They are an embarrassment, so we ignore them.

But we deal with the important things, don't we?

Our media four-walls a song-and-dance man, and news shows and the president anoint him an icon, a hero, a great American; we pay tribute, design memorials and televise our outpouring of grief and concern for this pop star who supposedly had a bad childhood.

And those we sent to war as teenagers and who came back maimed physically or psychologically are just a fact of life that we more fortunate ones have to live with, preferably in silence and darkness.

We don't like seeing them, so we close our eyes or put them in the closet.

There have been no trillions of stimulus dollars spent caring for our veterans. We use that to bail out those whose greed devastated the life, liberty, and pursuit of happiness our veterans secured for us.

We go into the worst national debt we have ever seen as we pay out hand-over-fist to those miscreants who caused "we the people" to lose our homes, jobs, retirement funds, health benefits, and nearly toppled the world economy.

But for those who walk the streets with post-traumatic stress disorder, with addictions they learned while fighting for our country, we do only enough to get a few votes — only enough to tell ourselves we tried.

Thousands take to the streets to immortalize a man who admitted bringing children to his bed for sleepovers. Thousands express their outrage that, "He never had a chance to be a child."

And if we can find it in our collective hearts to do that much for a pop star, maybe it is time for the American people and the American president to put up or shut up.

Maybe it is time to take care of those who defended our freedoms. Get them off the streets, into jobs, off drugs and alcohol, and back into the lives they left when they went to our wars.

Or be truthful and add these freedoms to the Bill of Rights:

1. The right to ignore our defenders.

2. The right to allow them to die hungry and cold in the streets.

3. The right to close our eyes when we pass them in winter morning doorways.

4. The right to send the next batch of sons into the same Stygian hell.

In 2009, immigration became front and center, and half the TV audiences were lied to about how they differed from our ancestors who had come here as immigrants.

He wrote about the lies about immigration:

"Among the stories told about my grandfather, Cornelius O' Connor himself, there is the one that he was, at one time, affiliated with a group in New York called the Dead Rabbits. I heard about that when I had barely reached the age of reason. I don't know if I believed it then because it was such a strange name for a bunch of Irishmen, but then I saw it take life in the 'Gangs of New York' so now it has a little more credence.

There was another oft-told story that came back to me the other day when Vivian and I were having breakfast at a cafe in Shelton.

Three men at the counter were talking about immigration, and one of them said, 'We all came from immigrants, but ours came here the right way. They came legally. That's why I don't want these new ones, these Mexicans, and Arabs, and Indians. They come here illegally. They should be thrown out like we used to do.'

Oh really?

Before the turn of the century, when a young Irish farmer from Skibereen boarded a boat in Ireland, he had no idea that his name was about to multiply during a long ocean voyage.

It seems there was a Cornelius O'Connor, a farmer, and there was the other man, the one he met on the way over. This other man was running from the English law. He was considered a political outlaw and, as my father used to say, "a very rough and tumble man."

He too was a Skibereen man, and that is how they met. As they approached New York and the new world, and dreamed about making a brand-new life, they hatched an idea.

The story goes that, even at this time, when only about 1 percent of those who made it to Ellis Island were turned back, and most of those were Chinese, the two were afraid there might be someone waiting for this other man, ready to arrest him and take him back to an English jail, or not.

No one, however, was looking for Cornelius O'Connor, a farmer. They both took the same name and queued up to leave the boat. One, it was said, was in the front of the line and the other way to the back.

They expected with so many Pattys and Corneliuses, Michaels, Seans and O'something-or-others, two Cornelius

O'Connors wouldn't be such a big deal, but they felt a little space between them wouldn't hurt.

They both made it to the shore. They both made it to the city. They both made it to the new world. They went their own ways. One of them was my grandfather. We don't know for sure which one.

Back then there was no social security number. When I hear that our ancestors came here legally, I have to laugh. There were so few legal rules they had to adhere to in order to come to the United States. Unless they were Chinese — because it was deemed that Chinese looked too different to be assimilated into American life.

So please, when you think your ancestors were a different ilk from the ones trying to come here now, please get a grip. A lot of them were not here legally. And although they may have been good people, a lot were even considered criminals in their own countries. This is a country of immigrants, many of them illegal.

We can search for all the excuses we want to stop new immigrants from coming here, but to say our forefathers came here legally is blarney. Of course, we could just say they may not assimilate, like we did to the Chinese in the 19th century.

It's the same thing. The Irish could lose their brogue and become Americans, but Mexicans, Arabs, Indians have the *same problem as the Chinese did. They look different from what we see in our mind's stilted eye as Americans.*

In 2009, the country waded into its first forays into cancel culture. Say the wrong thing, lose your job.

He wrote about false tolerance:

"When the final books are written, I'm afraid the truth will be that we taught this generation tolerance means being careful what you say out loud about people you don't like.

It's alright, it seems, to be intolerant in deed, but if you admit to it, you have to lose your job to assuage our collective subconscious guilt or to minimize the damage to our pocketbooks. Ari Fleischer said the most important thing he ever said when opinion columnist Helen Thomas gave an opinion contrary to what we want to believe is the common perception of the rights of Israel.

For the record, when asked if she had "any comments" on Israel, she said, "tell them get the hell out of Palestine. Remember these people are occupied, and it's their land. It's not Germany... Poland. They should go home to Poland, Germany, and America and everywhere else."

Now, she may be wrong, but there are a lot of people in the world who agree with her. We could start with the Palestinians. But American tolerance this year only goes as far as saying good things about Israel. The truth is, Americans are always tolerant of Israel, but as an old boss of mine once said, "I wonder how we would feel if, instead of giving them part of Palestine, we gave them Rhode Island and parts of Connecticut and told everyone to get out. Let's see how tolerant we would be then."

Fleischer, who had been press secretary for President George W. Bush, said, "She should lose her job over this. ... As someone who is Jewish, and as someone who worked with her and used to like her, I find this appalling. She is advocating religious cleansing. ... If a journalist, or a columnist, said the same thing about blacks or Hispanics, they would already have lost their jobs."

He's right. They would have. Why? Because when it comes to intolerance, we don't mind seeing it, we don't mind it being done, we just want people to keep quiet about it.

For instance, the census takers of America wouldn't hire anyone who was ever arrested, even if the charges were dismissed. This discriminated against blacks and Hispanics since they are more apt to be arrested in this country than white people. The fact that minorities are more apt to be arrested, in itself, shows intolerance, but if someone said, "Stop stealing things, and you won't get arrested," that person would lose his or her job. Of course, the racial profiling that everyone knows goes into the initial arrest isn't seen as intolerance, unless we admit we're doing it.

The unemployment rate has always been worse for minorities, because the people doing the hiring would rather hire white people, I guess. But that isn't seen as intolerance unless the employer says out loud, "Hispanics need not apply."

And now it is the trend: We want to talk about racism in America.

I only hope we'll talk about all of it.

The truth is there are racists of every race, sex, country, and religion. The big difference in America is more white men control the jobs, the money, the badges, the schools, and the courts. Don't worry, that's changing.

The truth is only newcomers are allowed to preserve their culture. If the people who have been here a while try to preserve their culture, they are called racist.

The truth is most Americans are tolerant of homosexuals only until they leave the room, otherwise they'd be able to get married in every state.

The truth is that it isn't intolerant to make it difficult to become an American citizen. If it weren't worth the extra effort, people would be trying to sneak into your country.

Even the president says we should be tolerant of Muslims, and they should be able to build a mosque near ground zero.

Then some fool will probably blow it up because, right or wrong, the truth is a lot of people are a bit miffed about what happened at the twin towers.

The truth is that Islam doesn't seem to be the most tolerant religion in the world, but it is also true that the tenets of almost every religion are based on being intolerant of all the others.

You want to talk about intolerance? Go ahead, it won't change a damned thing.

We really should be aiming for tolerant actions, rather than worrying so much about intolerant words.

In 2009, the US, China, Brazil, India, and South Africa all agreed to work concurrently on global warming, and complaints about how our young people, who it was said had been given everything they wanted in life, had become obnoxious.

He wrote about redrawing the lines of civilization:

'The state of American civilization comes down to chewing gum.

Remember how we weren't allowed to chew gum in school and other seemingly stupid rules? Remember how we did away with those rules for our children, and they did away with others for their children?

It may have been a big mistake.

Every new generation chooses a lifestyle that tests its parents. It has always been the wont of a child to push the parents' limits. Raccoon coats and beatniks; black leather jackets and juvenile delinquency; long hair, love beads, and hippies; and now we have faces that look like they came out of a tackle box.

I say this after a particularly strange Independence Day weekend. My wife and I went to West Haven for the fireworks. The ordeal reminded me of advice from a friend. Don was the superintendent of schools in a town I used to cover. He explained, "Controlling kids has to do with where you set limits — what you will and will not allow."

He said kids will always want to push the envelope. "It's our nature," he said. "If I make a big deal of chewing gum in school, that is where the kids will test us, but if I allow that and draw the line at drinking on school grounds, that is where they will push the limit. .... If I throw them out of school for gum, they wouldn't even think of bringing alcohol or a weapon to school."

I thought of this as Vivian and I fought the crowds on the West Walk.

Some people in their late seventies huddled on one bench, while two dreadlocked, twenty-something boys sprawled, each on his own bench, right next to them, staring up at the sky and spouting what sounded like lines from "Pulp Fiction."

No one thought to ask them to be quiet, or to let some of the old people sit a little more comfortably, and they sure didn't think of it themselves. I guess we, as a society, have chosen to allow this behavior.

I heard salted snippets of kiddie conversation spoken at a too-loud decibel-level for public. When I get to a word I can't print, which was every other word, I will use the word "puppy."

As cars rolled by, blaring a heart-stomping thump, thump and the lyrics about "puppy you" and "punching out the mother puppy female puppies," two young girls, about 15, stood right in front of me as one lamented that her "puppy father is a puppyhole." And she wished she could kill him. The skinny rat-boy she was clinging to wore a t-shirt that said, "I wish I could kill every day." Someone allowed that jerk to leave the house.

Some Goths walked down the center of the right side of the walkway, enjoying rerouting the crowd like parting the Red Sea. Six boys and a girl, and she was the loudest and filthiest, spewing verbal vomit at anyone walking by.

We set up chairs on the beach, an elderly couple to our right and a young family in front. Farther to our right were some young people, drinking and talking as if the beach were a bad bar.

When the fireworks began, they stood. We could see, but the elderly couple to our right had to move. Maybe they couldn't see what they wanted to or couldn't listen to what they had to. After the display, the young people to our right began firing roman candles aimed directly at the old couple, and when someone in the group pointed it out to the alpha puppy who was lighting them, he said "puppy them. Let them move. It's the puppy Fourth of July, dude."

I think we've drawn the line miles short of civility, and too many of our young people have lost all contact.

Isn't it time someone redraws the lines of civilization?

In 2009, immigration reform became the word of congress, and states on the southern border fought back.

He wrote about illegal aliens:

"Here in New England, we don't understand border problems the way those in Arizona do, unless we are talking about the Canadian border, and since Canadians have jobs and health care, they don't come here illegally looking for work to feed their families?

But what if Canadians began showing up in larger numbers than ever before? They take all the jobs available.

Then when the jobs are gone, some go home but some stay and make money by stealing it. The Canadians clog up our emergency rooms, and they send their kids to our schools. Then some of the Canadians even have kids here and they are born American citizens.

Suppose the police are nearly helpless to stop the Canadians because they have no specific laws to go looking for these illegal aliens who are taking jobs, stealing stuff, and bogging down our services. Suppose 70 percent of the American-born people here in the Northeast supported a new law that said cops could stop anyone who looked like an illegal Canadian.

Would we call all New Englanders racists?

No.

Look, seventy percent of the people in Arizona are not racists, either. Sure, some of them are, but not seven out of ten.

I lived in Phoenix when I was a kid, and the people I met there were proud of their mongrel status. We were from every state in the union and pretty much every country in the world.

According to census data, if every white person in the state of Arizona was in favor of this new law that would only be about fifty-eight percent.

Thirty percent are legal Hispanics, and the others are lower than five percent.

This means there are at least some minority residents who are in favor of this law, since seventy percent of Arizonans supported it.

Why? Because the old crutch, "Illegal aliens only take jobs that Americans don't want," is bull feathers.

We have people in this country standing in line in a driving rain for seventeen hours for the chance to get a job application to fix elevators. We have teachers working at supermarkets and accountants working in fast-food restaurants.

Arizona is believed to have an estimated 460,000 illegal immigrants and approximately 6.5 million legal residents. That's one illegal immigrant for every fourteen legal residents.

The people of Arizona have a right to want their government to do something.

Even with that said, I believe any thinking human being has to take exception to this new law.

A law that leaves it up to the police to decide who might be an illegal immigrant by looking at them is ridiculous. Hispanics are up in arms throughout the country saying they believe it will lead to profiling and racism. I think it is even worse than that.

In the beginning, police will stop Mexican people and ask for their papers. Then everyone who has dark hair and dark skin or who lives in South Phoenix will be stopped. My sister would have been picked up every day and questioned. My Irish father would not have stood a chance with his black hair and tanned skin from walking home daily in the desert sun. Even the Mexican kids who lived next door always ran out to greet him. He looked that much like their father.

Then southern Italians would be suspect, and African Americans, and American Indians (now would that be just the worst insult, profiling the only people who were actually native to this country because a cop felt they looked like illegal aliens). Then police would find out they could stop any car they wanted and as justification they say, "I suspected the inhabitants were illegal aliens." So much for probable cause.

I believe being a cop is probably the most difficult job in the world. Their hands are so often tied by our guaranteed freedoms that they have to be almost certain a crime has been committed before detaining someone.

True, if we could suspend those guarantees, it would be an easier job, but it isn't supposed to be easy.

If the federal government made the process of becoming an American citizen a little more rational, those who find it necessary to come to feed their families would do the right thing, become citizens, obey the rules, and pay their taxes.

Although something is needed to protect the citizens on our southern border states, this law isn't it.

In 2009, a new more intense form of partisan politics raised its ugly head to nullify the new black president.

He wrote about the danger of the plausible opposite:

The Pledge of Allegiance says we are "one nation, under God, indivisible."

Oh, no we are not.

An 1858 speech by President Abraham Lincoln said, "A house divided against itself cannot stand."

That you can believe.

And that is why our country is on one knee and wobbling.

Our most devastating problem is not war, or the economy, or health care, or corruption.

It is partisan politics.

Beware the probable opposite.

No matter what one party sees as an answer to a problem, the other immediately presents us with a probable opposite to shout them down and grab back power.

Truth is of no consequence to them as long as it is probable and therefore believed by many of the wavering and all of the fools.

Mark Twain said of democracy, if you have all the fools of the country on your side, you will win because don't the fools outnumber the rest of us and are therefore a majority in any instance?

The probable opposite convinces fools.

The president currently is a Democrat. If he were a Republican, the roles I am about to talk about would be reversed. The respective national committees are the ones designated to formulate the probable opposite.

Take health care reform.

The president points out that our health-care system is run by insurance companies who are looking for profit over humanitarian efforts. He says he would like to change that system to allow everyone to have health care. He says a little competition couldn't hurt the corporations now in charge and proposes a government-run competitor to even the playing field.

The opposition immediately says: This puts the government in charge of your health care. This is bad, they say, and the probability that the government will be worse than insurance companies is swallowed like a very expensive pill. They say the government will then be killing children through abortions.

This is not true, the fact finders say, but it doesn't matter.

They say illegal immigrants will be paid for. Not true, say those who find facts.

Then they say the most incredible thing: If this plan goes through, Democrats won't let Republicans have health care. Preposterous, but believed by some. And the foolish tide starts to turn.

A TV commercial arrives that says, now that the new health care plan has:

"No guarantee that you won't wait longer at the doctor's office. No guarantee that the cost will go down."

Those carefully crafted statements, and the others that follow, are designed to fool non-thinking people. They could just as probably say there is no guarantee the Democrats won't kill your first born, or steal your car, or come to your house and kick your dog.

Then the President does something no other president has done.

He addresses all the children returning to school this year. Opposition critics say he has overstepped his authority, that he is just trying to further a political agenda.

He tells kids to stay in school, study hard, and make something of themselves, and we have to hear the probable opposite. That he is somehow trying to proselytize our children for the Democratic party.

I am not blaming just Republicans. If there were a Republican president, the Democrats would be doing the same. They have in the past.

If any president, at any time in recent history, said there was enough food to feed the whole country for free, that all you had to do was go to the store and pick up what you want, and that it would continue forever, the probable opposite might be, He is just trying to buy votes.

Why is it that the only time we ever get a near unanimous vote in support of any president — without the onslaught of the probable opposites — is when he calls for a war?

If we keep believing this nonsense, we will stagnate right where we are and watch our health costs rise and rise and rise until only the congress will be able to afford it.

Politicians have found out that if you say the probable opposite long enough, it becomes a false equivalency.

We must stop buying the talk-radio logic of the probable opposite as anything other than what it is — stuff you find in a political pasture.

In 2009, young people were under the gun for what appeared to be their bad driving habits, and it was being discussed that the driving age should be raised to twenty-one.

He wrote about the driving force behind teenagers:

"I have no solution for the problem I saw this past weekend, just respect for young people who negotiate the labyrinth we have given them.

It has to do with the insane changes our world has seen in just the past hundred years.

When my father was 17, a driver's license was pretty much optional, and a-mile-a-minute was about as fast as anyone wanted to go. He never bothered to get a license even though for years he made a living driving an oil truck.

When I got my license, I slept through a drivers-ed course, took on-road instructions from the one person in town who had the nerve to make a living teaching children how to drive a 4,000-pound, rumbling '56 Buick, and then I took a road test which was ultimately designed to make a person fail.

I really learned for the next year on deserted back roads driving a 41 DeSoto that could barely make forty-five mph and got about eight miles to the gallon.

I taught my kids to drive in a parking lot. Then they went on to a school-sponsored course and an expensive driving school which had classroom training and road training, part of which was on I-495 north of Halford, Massachusetts. At the time, it was a deserted road.

Then came last Tuesday.

Vivian and I took our last look at the waves off short sands beach in York, Maine, and got into the car around seven a.m. By eight, we were in New Hampshire. By ten, we were passing through Massachusetts, and by noon we were in Derby, Connecticut.

I thought back to what a four-state trip entailed when my father was a kid. It had to do with lots of gas money, sandwiches, and a few days at thirty mph.

On the way back from our mini-vacation, I noticed I was averaging about seventy-five mph in a tight formation of mile after mile of cars, trucks, and motorcycles. A nutcase on my bumper was the only time I slowed to about a-mile-a-minute, just to irritate him.

I have been driving for forty-six years. This is a lot of practice, and even I was tense in the middle lane at seventy-five with an eighteen-wheeler passing me on the right, a Statey on the left, and a clutch of cars as far as I could see.

There were enemy cars all around me a few feet from my plastic-encased body. There were ice holes between lanes even though it is August and eighty-five degrees. There were elevated highways, bridges, scarred roadway caution signs, uneven lanes (one three inches higher than the next), cowboy truck-jockeys in the fast lane, middle-aged men taking testosterone pills and flitting their Porsche in and out of traffic eyeing each car they pass for younger women.

For many of those on the highway, keeping your hands at nine and two has been replaced by keeping your hands at quarter of 12 and 12:15. How else can you steer while texting? There were women doing makeup at eighty and men babbling on their cell phone while drinking hot coffee, and the technically savvy were steering with their palms while sending messages to their friends about how crowded the highway is and how fast the traffic is going. OMG.

We stopped at a highway plaza, and there, having a cigarette outside the place, was a barefoot kid in camo shorts, a sleeveless T-shirt, and a tattoo on the side of his shaved head that said "No." He turned, and I saw the other side read "Fear."

Then, only a few minutes back on the road, I saw the most frightening thing I believe I have ever seen.

There, trying desperately to move from the middle lane to the slower lane to exit, was a Toyota Camry with a sign on the back declaring STUDENT DRIVER.

How do young people learn to drive on these roads? How does a seventeen-year-old, who learned most of his driving skills from a video game, handle this?

Long gone are the hometown back roads devoid of cars where young people can learn to turn a car or slow it down on a hill. Long gone is the steel-encased chassis that could take down a mailbox and a stone wall without so much as a dent.

Now we shove our pubescent kids into plastic jet skates with a GPS, a cell phone, a smart phone, earphones so they can't hear the traffic, and so many distractions they can't see it. We poise them on an entry ramp and kick their untrained butts onto I-95 with their newly acquired license to kill or be killed.

And when anyone suggests raising the driving age, it is the parents who are the first to complain.

I don't have a solution for this. I just want to say I have a newfound respect for the teenage drivers who manage to make it to voting age, and I am worried about the parents who would rather have them dead than drive them to school.

———

In 2010, bullying became a household word.

He wrote about bullying and school shootings:

I've seen a lot of bullying in my life, but it didn't end up the way it does now, with kids killing the bullies or killing themselves.

I think part of the problem now is that this new crop are not actually bullies. That is like calling murderers "a bit anti-social."

Persecution is the new bullying.

I think the biggest problem is kids are no longer taught that there are ways to handle a bully short of mass murder or suicide.

When I was a kid, my father taught me there were four ways to handle a bully.

1. Ignore him, he may go away. 2. If that doesn't work, avoid him. He may find someone else to bother. 3. If that doesn't work, go to the authorities. 4. If that doesn't work, punch him in the mouth. He may beat you up, but then he'll go find someone else to bully, someone who won't hit back.

Now, start with the fact that with the divorce rate over 50 percent, and with one out of three babies being born out of wedlock, we have around 50 percent of the kids in the country plowing through life without the benefit of a father.

Let me tell you a story about my stepdaughter Robin. She was being bullied at school. Not just verbal intimidation, either. I took her aside and told her what Scrapper Jack had told me. Then I taught her how to throw a punch.

She was a little girl and I didn't want her hurt, so I felt a little self-defense couldn't be a bad thing.

A week later, she was suspended from school for breaking a girl's nose.

It didn't seem to matter that she had been intimidated for months by this group of girls, or that at this particular time she was cornered in the school bathroom and the only way to the door was through the girl blocking it.

I was happy I had taught her how to get out. And the bullying stopped.

Then there was Carter. Carter was a polite and intelligent kid who was also the toughest tackler on my soccer team.

He was bullied in school by an older group of boys, and on one day he was followed down the hall and slapped from behind. He was hit in the head several times and then punched. He finally turned and physically made his tormenter sorry he had started the fight. Carter was suspended from school because of some zero-tolerance nonsense.

I say nonsense because, as any thinking adult knows, zero tolerance policies for fighting are only so teachers and administrators won't have to try to figure out who was right or wrong, punish everyone and be done with it.

In Carter's case, I was told by the principal, "There is never a good reason for violence."

I said, "How about WWII?"

He didn't understand.

So why is bullying coming to such horrible ends now: Kids killing themselves or assaulting entire schools with automatic weapons?

I have a theory.

First, there are far fewer fathers at home teaching kids how to handle a bully. And even if kids now had the same advice I got, it wouldn't work.

You can't ignore bullies anymore, and you can't avoid them.

They are still present in school, but when you go home, you are no longer safe. Social media interaction for the most part in today's kid society takes place on the internet, or on the cell phone, or some other high-tech device, so kids are always vulnerable to bullies.

And in most current cases when the persecuted kid goes to the authorities of the school, they do nothing.

They tell themselves bullying has always gone on in schools and kids must learn to deal with it. Well, the way we dealt with it is no longer an option because authorities will pay no attention to you when you ask for help, and they'll punish you for defending yourself.

So, the persecution gets worse and worse and continues and builds until the kid being bullied can no longer take it and kills himself or herself or kills whoever was bullying them.

You want the bullying to stop?

Teach kids there is a way to handle it short of automatic weapons or a noose, and then back them up when they do it.

Bullying is not a kid problem. It is an adult problem.

In 2010, a resurgence of priest flogging hit the airwaves.

He wrote about the attacks on priests:

"I have to ask. Just once. And every nutcase and outraged

journalist in the world is going to email, or write, or phone to tell me how wrong I am.

I don't care. I'm going to ask anyway.

Haven't we all had enough fun flogging Catholic priests for being almost as depraved as the rest of the country?

When does this stop?

I'm told about three percent of the priests in our city and less than two percent of the priests worldwide have been involved in accusations of sexual abuse, most of it thirty-five to forty-five years ago.

Let's get some more opinions on that.

History and religious studies professor Philip Jenkins of Penn State University estimates that two percent of priests sexually abuse young people.

Another?

Richard Sipe is a psychotherapist and former priest. After about forty years of studying the problems, he estimates that six percent of priests abuse and only two percent abuse "pre-pubertal" children.

Attorney Silvia M. Demarest has been tracking accusations against Catholic priests for almost twenty years. She says about two and a half percent have been accused of abusing young people.

A survey of sexual abuse of children within the church

issued in February 2004 estimated that four percent of the 110,000 priests who served between 1950 and 2002 were abusive.

Try to remember that there are some people who haven't come forward, there are others who have "remembered" repressed memories that may or may not have ever happened, and some are just plain lying. We may also do well to remember that even if you take the largest estimate, six percent, that means that 940 of every thousand priests have not even been accused of it. Go with the lower end of two percent, and 980 of 1,000 are without sin.

But we keep throwing stones.

A study done by Santa Clara University says five percent of Catholic priests have a "predilection toward minors," while the general population seems to be around eight percent.

So why is it we are still beating on the entire priesthood?

Seems we did the same with Boy Scout leaders and teachers for a while, but not nearly as long.

I spent my first thirteen years in close proximity to priests at a Catholic School, as part of an Irish Catholic family. I never, never heard anything about pedophile priests. If it was going on, I would have heard about it. Kids talk.

I left St. Mary's in the early 1960s, and it seems that in the 60s and 70s there weren't a lot of people begging to get into the priesthood.

But parishes had to be administered to, and it seems that some who were accepted out of necessity had heard the call of a different god.

The accusations against priests spiked in the 1960s and 1970s, but since then have returned to the levels of 1950.

The past two popes have apologized and established new standards and rules in hopes of stopping the abuse.

People seem to have forgotten that in the 60s and 70s, when most of this was happening, it was the prevailing thought, not just in the church but in all of society, that the way to handle sexual abusers was with counseling, not prison. The Catholic Church was not the only one doing this.

So here is what we have.

A miniscule percentage of the priesthood has been accused. Most likely, an even smaller percentage are guilty.

The Church leaders have apologized and compensated accusers.

Standards and procedures have been changed.

Accusations are being handled differently by the Church.

I am not saying this stuff didn't happen. Enough have been proven guilty to show us all that it did. But not all of those accused did it.

I guarantee that.

And if the Church did hide and protect those who were accused instead of investigating them and sending them to court, I feel the Church did something wrong — just as most of the country did something wrong in similar circumstances at the time.

If you have been abused, file your suit, go to court, and try the case. And if the priest is found guilty, put him away. He deserves it.

But in the meantime, at least remember that better than nine out of ten priests are good people who are being flogged daily for no reason, and I ask: When does this stop?

Enough is enough.

In 2010, false tolerance brought about the idea to put a mosque at Ground Zero.

He wrote about the growing ignorance in the country:

The world has gone stupid.

Here in Connecticut, a school graduation was to take place at a church hall. It was cheap and large. But the judge says no. It made kids feel uncomfortable to see symbols of someone else's religion. I ask, if there are kids so insecure in their beliefs that the mere sight of someone else's religious symbols makes them uncomfortable, I think the fault, dear Brutus, may not be in the stars but in ourselves that we are how we are.

People of the Westboro Baptist Church, based in Kansas, go to the funerals of American soldiers with signs that say, "Thank God for dead soldiers," and "God hates fags," and instead of having the police throw them out or allowing the parents of the deceased to pummel them with their own signs, we sue, and forty-eight states and the District of Columbia submit a brief to the Supreme Court supporting the lawsuit against the protesters, but Virginia and Maine decline to sign it.

As ignorant as it is for these malignant intellectual dwarves to be at funerals with their stupid signs, it is dumber still that there are whole states of people who seem to show by their inactions that they feel it may be okay.

An oil rig blows up and falls into the ocean, spewing oil into the Gulf of Mexico, destroying the ecology and economy of the region, and some people believe it is the fault of the President of the United States. To them I say, "Yup, it's all his fault, and you are perfectly sane."

In Albany, New York, a thirteen-year-old boy goes to school wearing a rosary. He says he is wearing it to remember his younger brother who was found clutching it when he was killed after a bicycle accident. The school assumes he must be lying, and that the rosary is in fact a "gang symbol." He is suspended. It is going to court. And we wonder why our kids are not the cream of the crop when compared to their peers across the world, and I say it is probably because some of the people educating them are stupid.

We now have a proposal for a mosque to be built two blocks from Ground Zero.

What?

Building a mosque in the shadow of Ground Zero is the single most insane thing I have heard in my lifetime. You figure it out.

Now, the world is up in arms because Israel boarded a ship that was running its blockade of Gaza and some people were killed.

I have a question. What on earth did you expect? It's a blockade. It started because the people who run Gaza were lobbing rockets into Israel and killing people.

This dumb epidemic isn't run-of-the-mill stupidity like we used to have. This is university-level. It would take an entire team of psychiatrists just to scratch the surface of how we got so stupid.

Here's an example of the type of stupidity I'm talking about.

I had a dream where I delivered a package to a store, and when I looked outside, I saw that my car had been stolen. I dialed 911 to report the theft.

"What's the address?" asked the cop.

Now here is what I consider the type of stupidity I believe has taken over the world.

I asked the owner what the address was. He laughed at me and called me a fool. It was my dream. If I didn't know the address, the characters in my dream didn't either.

A rosary is a gang symbol, therefore ban all rosaries from school.

Soldiers die as punishment for homosexuality, therefore it is okay to picket their funerals.

The president caused the oil spill; therefore we should vote Republican next time.

There should be a mosque at Ground Zero to show how tolerant we are of the people who blew it up in the first place. (I know all Muslims are not terrorists, but I still don't hear the outcry when their more radical fringe blows up a coffee house or a plane or our twin towers.)

It is okay for Israel to have a blockade; they just shouldn't be able to stop people from running it?

If kids are uncomfortable, we should move heaven and earth to make them comfortable.

I believe all these things are about as stupid as asking a character in my own dream to tell me something I myself don't know and expect an answer.

My question is, should opinion columnist Helen Thomas lose her job for having given her opinion?

In 2010, the country was facing a possible depression if the new president couldn't avoid it.

He also wrote in late 2010 about the creeping outrage in the country:

The depression of 2010 frightened the greedy fools who caused it more than the rest of us.

I'll tell you why.

It reminded me of a half-painted plank that rose up the side of the stairway at Depot Shoe where I used to wait for my old man so we could walk home.

This particular day, I didn't see him coming until he was sitting right beside me.

"This is a good idea," he said, hunkering down. "The stairway keeps the wind off you." He admired my ability to keep warm in a Salvation Army cloth jacket.

It was a comfortably brisk fall day, so we decided to sit awhile, and whenever we sat awhile, he told stories. After all, he was true Irish.

This day, he told of a train ride he took in the 30s across the dust bowl and into California looking for work in the fields. He also told of the conductor who threw cans of peaches off the back of the train as it rumbled through the tent cities, lulling the hobos to sleep through the fear of the smell of kerosene. "And Jocko," he said, wide-eyed, "the adults scrambled for the cans like kiddos, with no reservations and only what pride the times had left them. They groveled in the cinders and the dirt beside the tracks to get a fair share of food."

He took out his Luckies, tapped one on a thumbnail to tighten the tobacco, then offered me one by holding the pack in front of me. I laughed. He did too because he thought it was a joke — thought I didn't smoke because I was only ten years old.

He went on to tell of Woody Guthrie, his favorite. (Could be why he became a union organizer later in life.)

"Woody would stop in the camps or in the factories and sing his songs until they threw him out. He'd be singing 'Birmingham Jail' and 'This Land is Your Land' and songs about hobos and drifters and unions. He told of workers just like us who were killed in a plane crash in a place called Los Gatos, and no one even cared who they were, Jocko. He told of beatings and the unbeatable spirit of just plain folk who had hard lives just like us."

Scrapper Jack had been lied to, and there were no jobs where he had been sent. "But I met a guy in a bar," he says, "who said Contadina was hiring, so we hopped a train and rode on to the fields. The guy who did the hiring was from Halford, and he gave me a job. Turned out it paid less than he said, but I got to send some home to your mother and the girls."

These stories must be why I grew up praying to be a hobo at Halloween. They were my heroes. The hardened men, women, and children who worked the fields and for whom there was no free lunch, even when it was "free."

He was out there long enough for his clothes to change colors where he sweated the most, and then jobs opened up in the shoe shops back in Massachusetts, so he came home. And he brought with him the stories of the last depression, of Woody and the road and sang his songs to us every night. I rode along with him and Guthrie and absorbed a unique understanding of the ways of the world. An understanding I hoped would never come in handy.

At the turn of the century, it seemed it might.

As he flipped away his cigarette in the practiced way a working man does, he said (and he would say it maybe a thousand times more before he died), "Jocko, if you got your principles intact, I've always said, 'Deal me your hardest card, I'll win this gorram game.'"

I never knew it was a sort of quote from Woody Guthrie until decades later, but I wasn't surprised.

Nature and greed got the country into it then, and greed got us into it again. But the real men and women will always survive.

Hard times breed hard people. It's the ones whose greed has made them soft who lose that game.

You can bet on it.

Also in 2010, he wrote about the Tea Party, and although the column received a first-place regional award for journalism, it was the last column he was allowed to write.

"I have questions about two words. I no longer understand them. They are 'patriot' and 'Christian.'

In our beginning, 'patriots' were men who espoused a violent revolution against an oppressive king.

Then, later, a 'patriot' was a person who believed in America — her freedoms and her rules.

Now, we have the Tea Party. They say they are to be called 'patriots' or 'Tea Bags.'

I hesitate to call people tea bags.

But I am not sure if I would want to call them patriots either, since I don't know what they mean by it.

Do they mean they believe the country is ruled by the iron fist of an oppressive king, who was elected by a majority of the people and can't squeeze his ideas through Congress with a shoehorn unless they are whittled, chopped, bent, and transformed into something he doesn't even recognize anymore? Is that what they mean?

If it is, are they suggesting and working toward a violent revolution? And if they are, shouldn't they be called 'traitors'?

I'm confused.

Or does 'patriot' mean someone who loves America and her freedoms and her rules?

If that is so, why would they grab their mass-produced posters and buttons and head out to protest every single thing said by the president of the United States? They can't hate everything he says, can they?

I certainly don't know any more what 'patriot' means, so I guess I will call them tea bags after all.

Then there is the word 'Christian.'

When I was a kid, it meant a follower of the religion founded by Jesus of Nazareth who taught 'love thy neighbor' and believe in a supreme being. He taught the worth of all people, that we are all brothers and sisters, and that love was the answer to everything. He even died rather than start a war.

Anyway, we now have the 'religious right' who call

themselves 'Christians.'

The more radical of them go to the funerals of soldiers with signs that say, 'Thank God for dead soldiers,' and 'God hates fags.'

They hate homosexuals and believe they should kill them.

Only a small step up the food chain from these miscreants are the Christians who believe murdering an abortion doctor is a good thing and understandable, even though Jesus believed 'vengeance is mine, sayeth the Lord.'

Then there are the other Christians who hate gays, Muslims, liberals, Jews, Hollywood, and Democrats. The southern Christians hate the northern ones, and the northern ones hate the southern ones, and everyone hates the ones from California, but there are only about fifteen of them, so it doesn't matter.

They refuse to render to Caesar the things that are Caesar's, and they understand why the poor aren't all that blessed and shouldn't be allowed to have affordable health care because 'it will come out of my pocket,' and they certainly seem to hate the idea that we have a black president.

I wondered if the new Christians understand that their founder was a left-wing, bleeding-heart, long-haired, pacifist Jew whose skin was probably darker than our president's and who taught that we were to love our enemies?

So now, while half the world is basking in the afterglow of Easter and the other half is taking pot shots at the pope, I found myself in a quandary.

What is holding these people from such diverse backgrounds together in the 'religious right' and the 'tea party?'

Then I saw her.

In the middle of a Tea Bag rally, an elderly woman with a stuffed monkey slung around her neck smiled vacantly as she walked toward the camera lens carrying a sign that read 'Send Obama Back to Kenya.'

Now, what's that got to do with patriotism or Christianity, I thought.

It was enlightening.

All I could hope for now was that this wasn't the glue holding this diverse group of people together — these new Christian patriots.

I could only have faith and hope the central and defining issue wasn't racism.

Because that is a word I do understand.

It has nothing to do with the others.

This turned out to be Kevin's final column.

The nation's growing ignorance, bullying, partisan politics, false tolerance, creeping outward outrage, the new lines of civilization, and the partisan politics of the Tea Party had caught up to him.

Before his next column was due, he was called in by the publisher who said there had been several complaints from advertisers who hadn't enjoyed his column, and within a few days he was told he would no longer need to write a column at all.

Kevin had been asking about how work from the paper had been sold to a group called Nexus, and he wondered if those who had written the work were being paid for it. The publisher asked Kevin to submit a bill for the work the paper had published. It seemed to Kevin that it was payment for something both he and the publisher knew was a raw deal.

CHAPTER NINE
Stepping Onto a Slippery Slope

———

In eight years, while Kevin's column had won fourteen state, regional, and national awards, he was sadly watching the deconstruction of America's local journalism.

As the readership dwindled and the advertising began to dry up in favor of social media, newspapers did a strange thing. They began to publish online for free. For years, it had been a joke. Now it was reality.

Somewhere around 1990, circulation numbers that were nearly at sixty million in the country began a downward trend, and by 2010 it had dropped to near forty million, and from there it was dropping fast.

The public didn't seem to care. One of the political parties began convincing the public that the fourth estate, the only thing that told people that their own party was lying to them, was the enemy of the people.

The corresponding "circulation" numbers for the internet were difficult to count but were not making up for the downward trend.

Circulation, however, wasn't the only problem.

***

Robert Callahan sat next to Kevin in the newsroom. He was about Kevin's age, had very dark hair, mustache, and goatee, and he was a big man who had been an editor on a different newspaper until the local paper he had worked for went under, and its talent was assimilated by the Tribune.

"You ready?" he asked Kevin as he picked up his lunch from his desk.

"I am," Kevin said, grabbing his insulated lunch bag. Sitting across from each other at a corner table in the cafeteria, they talked.

"They're going to bring the weeklies in here to be laid out," said Robert.

The new owners of their paper had also bought several weeklies and in combining the staff of all of them, the corporation had the chance to let some people go and cut the overhead of the paper.

"That's good, it will give us more work to do," Kevin said between bites.

"You know," Robert said, "I keep looking at the caliber of people they are bringing in. I don't see how they can replace us with them. I don't think they can do the job. I know that sounds pompous, but I really don't think they can do it."

"Oh, they can do it," Kevin said, dumping packet of stevia into his coffee.

"I suppose they could if no one cares about the quality of the product."

"They don't," Kevin insisted.

"Why would you say that?"

Kevin stirred the coffee for a few seconds and then said, "Did you see what happened yesterday?"

Robert squinted his eyes, and after a short time said, "You mean the new guy flipping out on you?"

"Right," Kevin said. "The new editor. Here's what happened. He told me I was to read the city stories and help with editing, so I was reading them, and I found that two different reporters were assigned the same story by mistake. They both wrote a story, and the facts were completely opposed to each other. One said A, one said B. The 'facts' in the story were opposites, and for all I know, they were both wrong because there was no proof of anything."

"Figures," Robert said. "Those damned alternative facts will get you every time. Who said you had to do that?"

"What?"

"Read the city stories."

"The new editor. He's got me doing the comics, the wire, the Wall Street Journal page, the business page, the real estate pages... and a couple of other things."

"Including the city stories?"

"Right, and the state stories. So I decided it might be a good idea to tell the new managing editor what happened."

"Because she had made the mistake. You want half of this sandwich?"

"No, thanks. Wait a minute. Who made it, you or your wife?"

"My wife."

"Okay." Kevin reached across the table for the sandwich. "Right, she is the one who assigned the story to two different people. So, I walked over to her desk and told her, 'You got two stories about the same thing that say totally different things happened.' She says I should mind my own business."

"What?"

"Right, she says 'I think you should be paying attention to the wire, don't you?' I told her, 'I just thought you ought to know that we were about to print something that contradicted ourselves.' So, the kid…"

"What kid?"

"The dufus with the half-assed mustache, he sits next to her desk, so he decides to be her knight in white satin, and he says to me, 'Kevin, I think you have been told what to do. I think you should do it.'"

"He said that? To you? Who the hell is he?"

"I don't know. I think they just put him into Mison's job. I think he's in charge of rewriting press releases from government offices. Anyway, I ignore him and tell her again she needs to deal with the two stories, or we are going to look like idiots, and he stands up and faces me and says, 'I think you should go back to your desk.'"

"He said that?"

"He did."

"So, what did you say?"

"Well, I told him, 'You're out of your league,

lightweight. Sit down and go back to your silly ass work.' He made a beeline for the editor's office to tell on me."

"Why?"

"Because he is a child and that's what they do. They tell on people. Then I turned to her and said she really should take care of the problem."

After a few bites of his Healthy Choice meal, Kevin returned to the story. "The editor called me in and asked me why I had called dufus a lightweight. I said, because he is, and I guess I'm getting used to telling the truth."

"What did he say to that?" Robert asked, laughing.

"He says, 'He is your colleague.' So, I said, No he's not."

Robert was fully laughing now.

"He said, 'of course he is,' and I said a colleague is typically a coworker in the same profession that has a similar status."

"He said, 'He is a similar status.'"

"I pointed out that we were 'probably of similar rank but not status.' He doesn't even know that we can't publish two diametrically opposed stories about the same thing in the paper in the same edition. For Christ's sake, that's double think. Holding two opposing ideas in your mind at the same time and believing both."

"Oh," said Robert, "I guess that's when he started shouting?"

"Right," Kevin said and laughed. "When he took a breath, I asked, 'So, you think I should go tell her it's okay to print both stories?'"

"What did he say to that?"

"He said, 'Get the fuck out of my office, and don't do that. I'll take care of it.'"

Both men returned to their lunches and after a while, Robert asked, "How long do you think we have before they let us go?"

"Don't know. Can't be very long. I'm thinking mustache is making about half of what I'm making."

"And probably knows a quarter of what you know."

"Six months," Kevin said back over his shoulder as he began returning to his desk.

"What?" Robert asked.

"Six months to a year," Kevin said, "but I wouldn't count on the year."

When Kevin arrived back at his desk, his new boss was waiting for him. The newsroom called her Rainbow Bright. She was an intelligent twenty-two-year-old whose only other job before being in charge of the layout of all the weeklies was editor of one of the weeklies that had been absorbed by the city paper.

"I have a new list of what we need to do. It's our new goals," she said.

Kevin took the paper and sat down. He read it. It was a list of impossible goals designed to make whoever was laying out the weekly papers look bad enough to be written up.

"Right," he said as he handed it back to her. "That's a bull shit list. It's a list of things that can't be done, so when it isn't done, everyone will say we haven't met our goal, and someone will get fired. It's a bull shit list."

Kevin turned to his computer screen and began to work.

He heard his boss sniffling as she left his desk area, and out of the corner of his eye, he saw her head straight for Dick, the man who oversaw all of the layout desk.

Within minutes, she was back.

"Would you come with me?" she asked and turned on her heel and walked off toward the conference room.

"Oh-oh," Robert said, and the two men with their combined seventy years of experience laughed.

Inside the conference room, Rainbow Bright sat proudly at the head of the table, shuffling papers and staring at them as if shuffling was at that moment the most important thing in her life. Dick entered the room behind Kevin, nodded to him, and sat down. Dick wiped his bald head with his hand, adjusted his wire-rimmed glasses, and looked everywhere in the room except at Kevin. He looked like a man caught in the middle of two alternatives, and one side of it was his own job flapping in the wind.

"I need to talk to you about your use of foul language in the newsroom," Rainbow said.

"You do?" Kevin asked. "Really? What foul words did I use?"

"You said bullshit."

"I did, but what foul words did I use?"

She stared defiantly at the man in front of her, refusing to answer. She continued to stare. Kevin knew all he had to do would be to go along with this nonsense, and he would soon be let go as she built a file against him. He knew if he didn't go along with it, he would be let go sooner. But backing down to this child was going against everything he was made of.

Kevin had picked cotton as a ten-year-old child in the sweltering heat outside Phoenix, had, in the fifth grade, carried a knife for protection. He had spent three years in a war zone, fought through a divorce, had been threatened at gun point, and no matter how rapidly his chosen profession was headed downhill around him, he was not going to be intimidated by the unpracticed stare of a petulant child.

After a few nervous moments, Kevin turned to the other person in the room.

"Dick, you going to let this go on?"

Dick looked at the young woman, the designated boss of the weeklies.

"You said bullshit in the newsroom," she said. "I am going to have to write you up."

"Young lady, people swear in newsrooms. I was brought up by a piece-working bedlaster who swore between syllables. In the newsroom, the word *fuck* isn't even a foul word. It is punctuation. The word bullshit doesn't come close to being foul. Dick, I'm surprised at you. I didn't expect you to be so fucking obvious." He turned back to the young woman. Her face was beet red. Kevin had assessed the situation and now knew it was expected that he would lose his temper and give her some reason to fire him.

"Yes ma'am," he said. "I spoke foul words in the newsroom. That is just not professional, so I will rectify my language and be a good boy. Write it up. May I go back to work now?"

She had no idea what to say, so she said, "Yes."

When he got back to his desk, he said to Robert, "I think six months might be a stretch."

It certainly didn't take six months for Robert, who died only a few weeks later. He had been a journalist and had worked until the week he died. He had once told Kevin about the man who worked in Kevin's chair before him. Robert had said, "He got sick one afternoon right after the meeting, and the next day his wife called in dead for him. Not sick, dead. You know, he won't be in today. He's dead."

The people at Robert's funeral, who were ready to fire him to get rid of his paycheck and the cost of his health insurance, spoke of the wonderful work he had done on the paper. They were right. He had done wonderful work on the paper, but they didn't really give a crap. They were about to fire him anyway, for being old, and sick, and for making a decent salary.

In 2008, including reporters, editors, photographers and videographers, there were 114,000 people working in daily newsrooms nationwide. By 2009, it was down to 104,000. Robert was one of those 10,000 lost. By 2011, it would drop to 97,000. Kevin was about to be one of those

17,000 who in three years had become unemployed.

The readership gave up on newspapers and started to receive their "news," or what sufficed for news, online or from each other in the corners of donut shops and bars across the country.

——

As the copy desk dwindled, Kevin's workload grew. He was even chosen to speak at a little league banquet hyping the news. It was a job the editor had taken on but found he had overbooked himself so he told Kevin he would need to fill in.

He was then assigned a few more weekly papers to lay out.

While the younger people on the desk were producing three to five pages a night, he was laying out ten to fifteen.

He knew he needed to find a way to avoid being the next one out. He was about ten months short of retirement age.

It wasn't really a personal thing. He made too much money, and he was being asked to train people how to do his job.

When he came into work one afternoon, he saw an email from human resources. He opened it and found it was a renewal form for his health insurance. He had been paying for "employee plus one" (his wife). At the very end of the email there was a place to electronically sign the contract and a condescending explanation that seemed a bit rude. It said, "To check this box is to sign this form. It will suffice as a contract. If you don't understand this, phone HR and it will be explained to you."

Kevin shook his head and checked the box.

At the end of the week, there was a meeting with not only the bosses from the paper all the way up to and including the publisher, but also some people from corporate.

After some meaningless drivel, two diametrically opposed thoughts were listed for the proletariat to hold in their minds and believe both opposites of how the paper was doing well and how there would be a round of layoffs soon. Then everyone was told how they no longer would be able to get health insurance for themselves and one other person. Instead, they would have to carry the much more expensive family plan.

Kevin raised his hand.

"Yes Kevin," the publisher said.

"I was just wondering something. At the beginning of the week, I got an email from HR that said I had to renew my health insurance. It asked if I wanted to change the limits or if I wanted it to remain the same. It also had this insulting nonsense at the bottom that insinuated I didn't understand that if I checked the box at the bottom I would be, in effect, signing the insurance form. It said if I didn't understand, I should call HR and they would help me."

"Okay, so?" the publisher asked.

"So, I checked the box that said Remain the Same."

"Okay." The publisher turned to the corporate visitors and smiled.

"No, it's not okay. I didn't get to my question yet."

"What is your question?"

"I was wondering, does that contract work both ways? I mean, it seems I have signed a contract that I will get the insurance I had last year, which was employee-plus-one. What do you think?"

The group at the front of the room huddled. After a full minute or so, Kevin asked again, "Do we have a contract?"

"Yes Kevin, it is a contract."

"I could call HR and have them explain it to me. So, it works both ways, huh?"

"Yes, it works both ways."

"For everyone?"

"Yes, for everyone."

After the meeting, he said to the young woman in charge of photography, "Let's see them fire me now. Be a great lawsuit. I noticed they had to honor our contract, so they fired me."

Being an older employee, who had gotten three percent or more in raises for nearly forty years, put him in a situation where every day was a battle to keep his job.

A few weeks later, Kevin had just returned from the daily meeting when a young black girl came to his desk and wanted to see a page he had laid out earlier.

"Can you call it up.?"

"I'm in the wire," he said. "Can you wait a second?"

"Are you watching porn?" she asked loudly enough so several people near them turned around, and she laughed.

"No. I don't do that," Kevin answered.

"You mean you don't do it here." She laughed even louder. Heads turned again.

That afternoon, Kevin complained to HR about the accusation. He was told a letter of reprimand had been put in the woman's personnel file.

This was all Kevin wanted. He just thought, for his

protection, it should be written down somewhere.

Only a month or so later, the young girl complained to Human Resources that she was working in a hostile environment. Several people, including Kevin, were named in the complaint.

When he asked at HR about the nature of the complaint against him, he was told it was about a basketball joke he had told to a co-worker that the young girl had overheard.

"Wait a minute," Kevin said to the HR person, also a young black woman. "This is what I said, and it wasn't a joke. It happened when I was in New Hampshire. My boss had told us about a black bear that was terrorizing his family at night, trying to get to his trash. I asked him what he had done about it. He told me, and I laughed at him. I said to him, 'You thought hanging your garbage bags from your kid's eight-foot basketball hoop was going to protect it from a black bear that was six feet standing on its hind legs? You thought that was going to keep him from getting it? Are you insane?'" He looked at the quizzical face of the HR woman for a second, and then asked, "What about that is hostile?"

The several men who had been named in the complaint were called into the editor's office about a week later.

"We are not going to fight this," the editor said. "No one is going to be fired, but she will be compensated, and letters will be placed in all of your files."

"I will," Kevin said.

"You will what?" the editor asked.

"I will fight it. I will not be called a racist when I'm not. Besides, she could just be pissed off at me for complaining about her pornography remark."

"What pornography remark?"

"You can read all about it in her personnel file. A letter was put in there according to Thaddeus and Dick. It explains the whole thing."

The editor looked at the HR woman at the end of the table. She shrugged and shook her head. "No," she said. "Nothing was put in her file about Kevin."

"We are not going to fight this," the editor said as a final word of the meeting.

"I am," Kevin said and left the room.

Kevin was busy for the next few weeks, doing his work and preparing for what he knew was coming.

Several days later, he was called in again. Everyone who was considered his boss was at the meeting.

Kevin knew it was best for everyone if they decided to fire him. They would save a lot of money and fill his position with someone who made considerably less. Because of his decades-long experience and the knowledge he had acquired over the years, the quality of a young replacement wouldn't be the same, but that didn't really matter anymore in this age of give the people what they want rather than what they need.

After an employee reached fifty years old, people in journalism had become expendable. Anything that saved money in the face of cuts in advertising and circulation was warranted, especially cutting the payroll.

At the meeting, Kevin brought with him a file folder that was about three inches thick.

"What do you have there?" the editor asked as Kevin sat down and put the file in front of himself on the table.

"A few things. I have saved all the daily assignment sheets that show since I complained about the ongoing situation, my job has changed." Kevin picked up the folder. "This paperwork shows that with everyone on the desk creating three to five pages a night, I am now assigned eight to ten a night, and that is just on the daily. I have also been assigned the eight to ten pages of a different weekly each night."

"Are you saying you can't do the work?" the editor asked hopefully.

"No. I am not saying that at all," Kevin answered. "The paperwork also shows I have been doing the work just fine." He pushed a small part of the paperwork he had amassed to the side and picked up another group. "This is the paperwork that shows I have also been given an additional assignment of editing the state and city stories, and the articles for the business section. This also started after I complained about our orders not to fight this hostile work environment situation."

Kevin pushed the new group of papers aside.

"Here." He pointed to the new group of papers he had just taken from the file. "Here, we have the assignment to edit and lay out the pages we use from the *Wall Street Journal* each week. This next piece of paper is the weekly comics that I need to lay out for Sunday, but of course I no longer need to write my Sunday column."

Dick had been fidgeting in his chair, and Rainbow Bright who had been poised to add her complaint to the mix now erupted.

"What?" she nearly shouted.

Dick took over. "Are you saying you think we are punishing you for complaining? Do you think we would do that?"

"And this small pile," Kevin added, holding up one

piece of paper, "is the reprimand for saying bullshit in the newsroom. You were there for that, weren't you Dick?"

The new editor sat quietly watching the show.

After a seemingly long silence, Dick said, "You will never convince me, or any of us for that matter, that you are being punished for complaining." He was looking directly at the new editor.

"I don't have to convince you," Kevin said. "I just have to convince six people who don't work here."

"I don't know what the hell you're talking about," Dick said with a nervous smile that looked as if it wanted to quiver. He too sat back in his chair.

"I do," said the editor. "Kevin, I understand. You can go back to work. The rest of you stay here a few minutes."

Kevin went directly to the desk of the young complainant. He pulled up a chair and sat next to her.

"You should be proud of what you did," he said. She looked at him quizzically. "No, I mean it. You should be proud that you stood up. But I want you to do something for me. When you go home, ask your parents about the fights people our age had to force the government to pass the Civil Rights Act. And ask them if there were some white people out in the streets with them protesting. You did a good thing, but for God's sake, know who your enemies are and who your friends are." He stood up and put the chair back where it had been. "No matter which way this goes, I'm proud of you." He said and went back to his own desk.

Kevin went back to work, and the next day, he stepped off the elevator and walked directly to Dick's desk.

"So, what have I done wrong while I was away?" he asked.

"It's not personal," Dick said, looking up for a moment from his paperwork.

"What?" Kevin asked quickly. "Did you say it is not personal? Did you really? Do you believe that? Do you believe it isn't personal when you go after someone's job? I have bills to pay. I have a wife to support. Her family is living with us now. I have them to support too. How the hell is it not personal?"

"It's just business." Dick looked at Kevin as if he actually believed it.

"It's fucking personal," Kevin said. "That's not what I stopped for. I wanted to tell you I have a little time on Tuesdays and Fridays. Is there any other work I can do for you?"

Within the next few weeks, Kevin had taken on several jobs no one else wanted to do, then came a day when the entire staff who worked on the weeklies, four of them, were out sick.

"I'll get you someone to help," he was told by his boss.

"No need," Kevin told her. "I'll lay them out and drop the proofs on your desk. If you could proof them and send them down to be plated, it would be good."

She agreed, and by the time the night was over, and it was time to go home, while everyone else did their fair share of three to five pages of work, Kevin had completed by himself his world page, three pages on the daily, and twenty-eight pages of the weeklies.

Each day, he asked for more work, and when he was finally doing the jobs of several people, he asked for a meeting with the publisher.

"I am going to retire," Kevin said.

"When?"

"In October. On my birthday."

"I have a few questions for you," the young publisher asked.

"Shoot."

"Did you really lay out thirty-two pages in one night?"

"Yes."

"Is that really the work usually done by six people?"

"Well, let's see. Right, five pages into thirty-two.

Right, six people."

"Did you really take only one day off for a heart attack?"

"Three days, but two of them were the weekend, and I don't work on weekends. That's what the people you are looking to fire in the newsroom do. We come to work."

"And now the most important question. When I was cooking hamburgers outside the building on the paper's anniversary, did you really go over to the welfare office and tell the people there to bring their kids over for hamburgers?"

"I didn't think you would mind."

"I didn't. I laughed when I heard about it. Good for you. October, huh?"

"Right, my birthday. Don't tell anyone until you need to, okay?"

The publisher agreed. They shook hands and Kevin stood up to return to his desk.

"Kevin," the young man called, standing behind his desk.

Kevin turned and said, "Don't say it isn't personal. Just don't say that."

"No. I wasn't going to. Sorry, but you had a good run, and we probably won't even be here for very long.

Newspapers are going to die soon. It's good you get to leave on your own terms."

He took on three more pages, and by the time Dick was told Kevin was leaving, Kevin was doing the work of five or six people. He had amassed every piece of work he could, and now the supervisor of the copy desk would have to disseminate that to a bunch of people who had no idea how to do it. It was Kevin's last salvo.

At his retirement cake party, he was called into the conference room where most of the newsroom had gathered around a huge cake with his name on it. They were all smiling as if they hadn't had his firing in the front of their minds for months.

"Speech," the young woman who was in charge of photography said.

"Well, if I say what I would like to say, I'm sure someone would call for security to usher me out. So, I'll just say, it's been real."

After a few silent minutes, Kevin spoke up. "No. I do have something to say. First of all, this party is pretty much typical for our comradery here. You have bought me the habitual going away cake, chocolate with butter frosting an inch thick on the top, and I have diabetes from the effects of Agent Orange. But you didn't know that. Of course, I have only been here eight years, so why the hell would any of you know that?

"You believe you are providing a noble service to the community. It used to be that way. We used to be adversaries of the government, and I know some of you are still doing your jobs expecting to be one of the checks and balances, but your mission in life as a journalist is nearly over."

Kevin sipped his black coffee and continued.

"In 1984, when I was just getting my feet wet in journalism, the circulation of daily newspapers in the country was about sixty-four million.

"By 2002, we had lost about ten million of those readers because of our own stupidity.

It's not your fault, well, not entirely. The reading public has demanded that real news be buried and the sensational news be shoved onto the front page. We wanted to keep our jobs, so we did what the readers demanded. They would only continue reading if we printed bad news and outrageous news. If we didn't print and broadcast what they wanted, they would stop reading and we would lose our jobs. They didn't do it on purpose. They didn't even know they were doing it. Then, even though we did what they demanded, they blamed us for the bad news. They say we are lost in sensationalism. That we are fake.

"We are fake. Not long ago, I heard an editor here say, right in this very room, how we are 'trolling for perverts.' I was told to get with the program if I wanted to keep my job."

Kevin cut himself a piece of cake. He watched as everyone ate their piece quietly.

"Well, we lost ten million readers doing that. Journalism is going downhill, and it's just beginning to pick up speed. We won't be getting the ten million back. They are going to the sensationalism that can be broadcast in a much more arrogant and partisan way on TV and on the internet in a hundred and forty characters."

Kevin now looked up and turned to the clutch of young people sitting together at the end of the table. "You all wasted your money on journalism school. You might as well go get yourself a better job. This one is over the crest of the hill, and it is going downhill faster and faster.

"Newspapers are done. It began with the local papers being eaten up by bigger papers, and then by bigger papers, and then we stopped covering small towns."

Thadeus spoke up, "Okay, that's enough. Everyone

back to work."

"Oh shut up, Thadeus," Kevin said. "This is my party." He turned back to the group of young-and-hopefuls at the end of the table.

"It wasn't long before the mid-sized papers were eaten up and the same stories ran in all the papers. It didn't matter what the stories inside were about as long as the ad space to news hole was sixty/forty. Now papers the size of even this one are sensationalizing everything. How many of you have been told it doesn't matter if you have the whole story, get it on your blog, get it on the website, and we can fix it later? All of you, right?"

Heads nodded.

"It will only get worse," he said. "No, it's not time to go back to work, Thadeus. The time to get back to work is long since past because of idiots like you."

Kevin got up and went back to his desk to put his things together. His fight was over.

Kevin was right. In 1970, there had been 1,748 daily papers in the country. By 2018, there would be 1,279, and two years later, by 2020, there would be 1,260. Also, in 2020, circulation of dailies in the United States had dropped to twenty-four million, and it was still falling.

In 2020 alone, three hundred newspapers closed, and between 2008 and 2022, the number of people employed in the newsrooms of the country dropped by fifty percent.

What was lost with it?

Small-town residents no longer even knew who their town officials were. Corruption in small-town government went unnoticed because it was never reported. Although the big city newspapers printed the big stories like supreme court decisions and national elections, they didn't print the problems with closing dilapidated mills in small towns. They made "educated" jokes about the presidential candidates but didn't see it when political henchmen were taking over their local elections. And there were no longer adversaries to local, state, and national governments. Rather than being an adversary, newspapers and networks had picked a side.

By 2022, people knew more about the war in Ukraine than they did about the property tax problems facing their own small towns because subdivisions had brought in so many new children and they needed to build a new school. They knew more about the Keystone pipeline than they did about the pollution in the river running beside their town wells.

Kevin sat at his desk. He knew all the people in the

newsroom were looking at him, wondering if anything would come of his final assessment of journalism. It was his last day. What could they do to him?

He thought, after having tried so hard for so many years to climb to the perfection of his profession, the standard had changed. It had been lowered — considerably — and he could stop climbing.

Those who hadn't reached the standard, for one reason or another, now had it reached down to them and cradled them into a comforting embrace of stupidity and its reciprocal under payment.

If you were better at your job than others, if you had decades of experience, you were worth more money and were therefore expendable. Spelling, grammar, talent, accuracy, and an inquisitive mind were all replaced by speed, and loyalty to those who read the paper was replaced with jaw-dropping sensationalism that left people saying, "How could people do that?"

Main line news now looked more like the tabloid nonsense that was formerly found at the cash registers of supermarkets with headlines such as Elderly Woman Eaten by Her Couch, or Hillary Clinton is an Alien.

The bottom line had become the top reason for existence.

Journalism wasn't to blame for all of it. They were,

after all, giving the readers what they wanted. Then the readership revolted against themselves and blamed it on "the media." Called them the Enemy of the People, and Fake News.

In 1984, the circulation of daily newspapers in the United States was sixty-three million, three hundred thousand. If the rule that five readers read every paper printed held true, that meant that every adult and teen in the country had access to a newspaper that was aimed at telling them what they needed to know to be informed about local, state, national, and international news. By 2020, only twenty-four million daily newspapers were printed, therefore only a third of the same population had access to a newspaper.

By 2002, the circulation of daily newspapers in the country was only fifty-five million. In 2004, it was fifty million. In 2011, it was down to 44.4 million. In 2015, only five percent of the population found out about the national election by reading a newspaper.

In 2017, daily newspapers had a national circulation of 30.92 million, and by 2018, it had dropped to twenty-nine million. In 2020, circulation had reached 24.3 million.

Journalism had become a pariah.

In 2007, there had been 73,810 employees in the nation's daily newsrooms, and by 2020 that had dropped to 30,820. Then between the time the COVID pandemic hit and 2020, six thousand journalists had lost their jobs, and of the 3,143 counties in the United States, 200 had no newspaper at all.

———

Small-town newspapers were being eaten up, swallowed whole, and regurgitated as advertising, being sold with a few sensational stories.

Readers, and those who turned to TV broadcast news and the entertainment networks that posed as news networks, still knew about terrorism. They still accused their opposition of war crimes. National politics became the pastime of the masses, and everyone joined a team, and as the Red Sox fans hate the Yankee fans, and the Yankee fans hate the Red Sox fans, everyone adhered to the forever rightness of their team and the wrongness of the opposition. Facts had no room to exist in the fight.

Republicans even complained about a Democrat president giving people money during a pandemic. They said it was just adding to inflation, and half of the people who might have starved if they hadn't gotten the money agreed because the president was on the other team. The southern borders of Texas and Arizona became table talk in Massachusetts and New Hampshire, and the lines of civilization were redrawn around false tolerance and the feigned outrage over things that didn't even affect us personally. The political parties became champions, and the two teams of the country went to war with each other.

People now knew the talking points that were drawn up in the bowels of campaign headquarters and swore to them without knowing any facts. And they didn't know what was going on in their own towns.

What was lost were newspapers printing police logs, court procedures, school board meetings, overzealous police budgets, elderly ladies who just wanted someone to paint their house. We lost the fourth estate. The country no longer had a check on the local governments, and we no longer had any idea of what was happening around us, in our own towns.

Small-town America missed it when the old proverb of elections resurfaced. "Don't worry about the voters, control the counters." No one told them about it, so they missed it.

Then local America lost its local watchdog, their local newspaper, and they couldn't care less.

They didn't even wonder why everyone took a side in things that didn't affect them personally, and what affected their own lives went undetected, unreported.

People complained about the eighteen-wheel trucks barreling through their residential neighborhoods but had totally missed the Zoning Board of Appeals rezoning to allow for the trucks to be housed there in what had always been a ballfield.

They complained about their ever-escalating property taxes but didn't bother to go to the School Committee meeting when the addition to the high school had passed. They didn't even know what had been on the agenda.

They dismissed entirely the meeting where the highway department was told to resurface the roads in the neighborhood of the chairman of the board of selectman but complained about the horrible state of the roads in their own neighborhoods.

They didn't know that the teenagers in their town had won a state championship, but they fanatically backed one political party or another with the rabid zeal of a mongoose attacking a snake.

The world literally became black or white, and Nazis and white supremacists crawled out from under their rotted logs and again roamed the streets of the nation's small towns enticing children to join their ranks.

The American flag became a symbol of racism, and of pro-police, the good ones and the ones who never should have been police to begin with. But no one knew the difference unless the story ended up on national TV.

The flag waved from the back of pickup trucks with AR15s in the cab.

Everyone had picked a side on the national or world stage, but no one knew what was going on in their backyards.

First, the television news became filled with fewer hard-nosed reporters and far more opinion celebrities. Instead of printing the local, state, national, and international news during the week and a few writers giving their opinions on Sunday, everyone had an opinion. But no one cared about whether the facts were true or not.

The country evaporated the eighth commandment.

Everyone was guessing at the truth. But still everyone picked a side, the facts be damned. The facts became "fake news" to anyone who didn't want to believe anything that went against their team's game plan.

And it all started right before the eyes of the public, when they should have stopped corporate conglomerates from buying up all the local newspapers and turning them into money-making trash.

And now, when they find something important and broadcast it or print it, the people who need to know what is being told to them laugh and call it fake news.

We all sat by and watched corporations become people according to the Supreme Court, then the corporation-people bought up congress. Then they bought the presidency, threatened congress with losing their jobs if they went against them, and had their man in the White House stack the Supreme Court with mindless sycophants.

And a free press wasn't there to stop them.

And all because we substituted "Thou shalt not lie" with "We are trolling for perverts."

The End

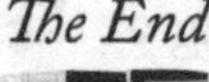

About the Author

John T. Hourihan Jr., a retired journalist, has won state, regional and national awards for his opinion column in several New England newspapers. He received the Cross of Gallantry for valor in Vietnam, where he served three tours as a Vietnamese linguist. He is disabled now from the effects of Agent Orange.

He lives with his author wife Lin Hourihan (*The Virtue of Virtues, The Mystery of the Sturbridge Keys*) in the woods of central Massachusetts. His other works include the Baltimore Catechism series: *Baltimore Catechism: The Fall and Rise of a Catholic Boy; Baltimore Catechism: Year of Confirmation; Baltimore Catechism: Mass of the Faithful;* as well as *The Mustard Seed – 2095, The Mustard Seed – 2110,* The Mustard Seed – 2130, *Beyond the Fence*: Converging Memoirs, *Parables for a New Age* I and II, *Play Fair and Win.*